THERE IS A COUNTRY

NEW FICTION

FROM THE NEW NATION OF

SOUTH SUDAN

EDITED BY NYUOL LUETH TONG

M^CSWEENEY'S

SAN FRANCISCO

www.mcsweeneys.net

ISBN: 978-1-938073-74-8

INTRODUCTION

by NYUOL LUETH TONG

When people learn that I am South Sudanese, they always have questions—not only about Sudan's long civil war and my opinions as to what might bring peace and stability, but about what kind of frame, or orientation, might offer them a more grounded understanding of this new nation. I am often asked to describe the literary culture of my country, and to recommend representative works. I understand why people would resort to literature, as opposed to media, to gain deeper knowledge about South Sudan; fiction and poetry can provide a sense of place that readers would otherwise have never been able to imagine.

I can name classics of American literature that have done just that for me. *Moby-Dick*, for instance, though a challenging novel for me in high school, owing largely to my then rudimentary English, has come to embody for me, over the last several years, exactly what historian Nathaniel Philbrick astutely calls "the genetic code of America: all the promises, problems, conflicts, and ideals." *Invisible Man*, *Beloved*, and *Blood Meridian* have offered me their own haunting glimpses into America and her history.

On the African continent, there is an international cast of writers whose works are powerful evocations of their cultural and social milieus. Chimamanda Adichie's *Half of a Yellow Sun*, Naguib Mahfouz's *Cairo Trilogy*, Chinua Achebe's *Things Fall Apart*, J. M. Coetzee's *Disgrace*, Tendai Huchu's *The Hairdresser of Harare*—these works, to me, are better vistas for understanding their respective countries than conventional historical accounts.

South Sudan, though, is still too young to be able to claim a literary coterie. Thus, when someone asks me for literature that illuminates its cultures and experiences, I tend to recommend personal accounts from my country's diaspora of former refugees and war survivors. I point them to books like Dave Eggers's *What Is the What*, a novel based on the life of Valentino Achak Deng; *They Poured Fire on Us From the Sky*, by Benson Deng, Alephonsion Deng, Benjamin Ajak, and Judy Bernstein; *God Grew Tired of Us*, by John Bul Dau and Michael Sweeney; *My Escape from Slavery*, by Francis Bok and Edward Tivnan; and *Slave: My True Story,* by Mende Nazer and Damien Lewis.

These works are all heartbreaking narratives of hardship and survival. They depict the horrors of war, the savagery of poverty, and the resilience, grace, and strength the human

spirit can assume in the face of utter desperation and evil.
Over the last several years, they have generated awareness
and support for South Sudan. They are testimonies; they
present hard evidence of the atrocities that occurred over
the last fifty years of turbulence. But I am reluctant to refer
to them as South Sudanese literature.

What, then, is South Sudanese literature? This question
evokes long-standing concerns about the nature of African
literature—its sources, its influences, its languages, its
possibilities—that writers like Chinua Achebe and Ngugi
wa Thiong'o have wrestled with in their deconstruction of
the colonial legacy. The need to find modes of expression
that suit African cultures and imaginings comes to the fore
here, charged with an urgency based in South Sudan's particular colonial context and current historical juncture.

In *War of Visions: Conflict of Identities in the Sudan*, his
seminal 1995 history of the nation, Professor Francis Deng
observes that "Historians have argued that without the
South there would be no North. This is even truer of the
South; without the confrontation with the North, the still
vivid history of rapacious invasions by northern slave raid-
ers, and the more recent attempts by the post-independence
governments to dominate the southern peoples, there would
be no South as a viable political entity." Today, according to Professor Jok Madut Jok, tension with the North
is still "the main glue that binds the country's multiple
ethnicities together."

The North has been painted as Islamic and Arabic,
while the South has been characterized as Christian and
African, and regionally part of East Africa; these are the
generalities that formed the discourse of the Sudanese
conflict, and of the eventual divorce. In reality, however,

hundreds of languages and ethnicities coexist in the
North. In the South, likewise, more than sixty languages
are spoken, and although both Islam and Christianity
are practiced, local belief systems dominate the spiritual
realm. Moreover, the last several decades of war have forced
millions of Southerners to flee their homes; many became
refugees in neighboring countries, but the bulk of the dis-
placed now live in slums and camps across Northern Sudan,
including in Khartoum, the capital.

South Sudanese culture, in other words, is a strikingly
hard to define thing. To further complicate our brief, all
of the stories collected here were written in English. As
Ngugi would phrase it: is this not "the final triumph of a
system of domination"? Or in Achebe's words: "Is it right
that a man should abandon his mother tongue for someone
else's?" English is not the main medium of conversation
for the majority of South Sudanese, especially in the
villages. That the first anthology of fiction bearing their
nation's name is in English, a colonial language, demands
an explanation.

The reality is that many people on the continent speak
colonial languages. In his collection of essays *Morning Yet
on Creation Day*, Achebe argued that "Colonialism in Africa
disrupted many things, but it did create big political units
where there were small, scattered ones before." These "big
political units" are united by common experiences under
colonial subjugation; colonial languages reinforce this unity
as a common medium of communication and of national
identification, an umbrella under which different ethnicities and cultures can find equal representation. English also
allowed many of the writers here to encounter literature
from elsewhere; it seems reasonable to use it to send our

own work out into the world.

This is the aim of this anthology. In an effort to enrich our culture and share the work of our new country, we want the world to read stories from South Sudan.

Finding these stories, were it not for the Internet, would have been virtually impossible. Apart from the acclaimed critic and poet Taban Lo Liyong, South Sudan's most well-known literary figure, and Arif Gamal, whose epic poem *Morning in Serra Mattu* is excerpted here, all of the contributors are young. I stumbled upon many of them while looking for African short stories online; others became known to me after our call for submissions went out, appearing from Juba, New York, Cairo, Nairobi, Sydney, London, Calgary.

I chose these narratives among the dozens received because they epitomize and illuminate South Sudan's current moment of rupture. Our nation has been marked by wandering and longing, by waiting and return. No other force or reality has had the ubiquity in South Sudan that war has had in the last several decades. War dominates, and its legacy will continue to influence our literature and culture in many ways for years to come. Its face is more familiar for most of us than this new reality of peace and stability. But there is more here, too, much more, and I hope that this collection will begin to give readers a picture of it.

ESCAPE

by EDWARD EREMUGO LUKA

The half moon was sinking slowly behind the dark rain clouds. The shadows melted into the corners of the compound as if a blanket had been spread over the land. In one corner, four tiny lights were shining. They moved. Black cats.

I stood at the door to my hut. The night was still new, but the town had already gone to sleep. It was quiet. There was no public electricity, and the few privately owned diesel generators in the neighborhood had gone silent. The children who had been singing next door had retreated to their homes.

The night weighed heavily on me, for it reminded me

that they would come for me one day. When they did, I would be ready for them. They have no faces, but I had a fair idea of who they were.

Juba, 1991. It was a terrible time for those who lived in that besieged town. The civil war had come to the largest city in the South. Residents could hear the rumblings of heavy guns and fighting outside town, and Juba itself had been shelled repeatedly. Casualties were being brought in as the Northern army suffered heavy losses.

As if to avenge their defeat on the battlefields, the Northerners brought terror into Juba. They were certain that the freedom fighters, the rebels, were hiding here among the civilians. They wanted to track them down, together with their sympathizers. The line between the guilty and the innocent was ignored.

When they come for me, I will be ready, I told myself.

I had become a light sleeper. I would wake up in the middle of the night and wait in the compound for morning. I was not trying to frighten away thieves hiding in the overgrowth; it was simply a good time to see the stars, flickering freely like innocent young children playing. It was a good time to think. The night breeze soothed my mind and enveloped me with calm. It was in these moments that I could strategize and plan.

A week ago, my close friend had told me that the faceless men were after me. It would be a matter of time before they pounced. I fit the profile of the wanted: I was well educated, a professional in my field of teaching, and had become popular in town. To them I was a suspect.

I had seen how countless others had been taken away in the middle of the night, never to be seen again. Families had been searching for their loved ones, but there was no one to give them answers. When you were taken to the infamous white house, to the detention cells, it was the last time you ever saw daylight. The place was incongruously named by Juba's citizens; everyone knew it was no luxury house. In fact, it was no "house" at all, white or otherwise, just a series of transport containers, some of them underground, where the Northerners kept their detainees. Few had come out of the white house alive. Instead they died from exhaustion, dehydration, or fear.

I knew many of the people who had disappeared. They had been picked up at night and tortured for information. The government's methods were extreme, and men would spout out the names of friends just so they could be released. Fear held people in its grip.

If I had to die, I wanted to die fighting. I didn't want to be added to the growing numbers of the disappeared; I did not want to join the decomposing bodies floating in the Nile, their arms and feet tied with wires and ropes. A relative of mine had found his father inside old Kenana sugar sacks that had been dragged from the water. They could only identify him by the clothes he'd worn the night of his disappearance. Everyone knew this was the work of the faceless ones.

The night was a hushed, haunted house. The usual barking of dogs and the slight breeze that swirled through the trees were conspicuously absent. The leaves were as stiff as rods. It was the perfect night for a raid, and I was ready. I was alone; I had sent my wife and children to stay with her parents. They would be safe there, at least for the moment. I knew that it would happen tonight, so I walked back inside. When I heard two knocks, I opened the door.

Johnny and Luambo slipped inside. Johnny was

breathing heavily; he had been running. His face was covered in tiny beads of sweat that glistened in the dim light. I turned the knob of the kerosene lamp to raise the wick and illuminate the room. Johnny sat down on the stool by the door.

Luambo was a big man with the full chest of a boxer. He worked as a mechanic at a garage in the Hai Malakal area. He walked over and sat on the bed. It squeaked loudly as the springs bore his heavy weight. For a few moments, nobody said a word. I knew this was not a social visit.

Johnny and Luambo were old friends. We had grown up together in the same neighborhood, gone to the same school; we had been inseparable. After we read Alexandre Dumas's *The Three Musketeers* in class, everyone started referring to us as Athos, Porthos, and Aramis.

Outside the hut, it began to rain. It was not the usual heavy rainfall, with winds and thunder and lightning. It was a light rain, which could last for hours without end. The kind that could fall all night. We loved this rain when we were young. We called it *seke seke*. When it started in the morning, it meant we would not go to school. We would remain at home, gathered around the fire in the kitchen hut, waiting for hot porridge seasoned with peanut butter.

It was Luambo, Porthos, who broke the silence. His voice, usually a strong baritone, was now subdued, almost a whisper.

"You have to leave tonight," he said.

"I'm not going anywhere," I said. "It is my home, my town."

"Listen to me," he said. "You cannot stay anymore. There is nothing to call home now. This is a war zone. You are a well-known and respected man here. You have already lost much of your family in this war; nothing is going to bring them back. No one can afford to lose you, too."

"But why do I have to run?" I asked. "We have prepared for this for a long time. I am prepared for them."

Johnny leaned forward. He had always been the quiet one of the trio. He spoke only to offer the final opinion and convince us all.

"No, you are not," he said. "They have already taken Thomas and Bambu tonight, and you know what that means. They know you met with those two a week ago. You were seen together."

Thomas and Bambu were two other friends that I knew very well. They had been working on a plan to resist the faceless ones. I had intended to fight with them, but now they were gone.

"They say a coward who runs away lives to fight another day," Johnny said. "You will have your time, Aramis."

There was silence.

"What happens next, then?" I asked.

"There is a man waiting for you at the end of the path near the cemetery," Johnny said. His voice was strong and firm. He had made all the plans. "He will take you to the riverbank, where a boat is waiting to take you across. On the other side, you will be met by guides who will take you to the road to Uganda. We have many friends who have gone ahead."

"You'll have to leave now," said Luambo.

"If they know I have gone, they will take you in," I said. I was making one last attempt to avoid going. "We have to go together."

"No. We cannot. It would prove that we were guilty,"

Luambo said. "You go. If it gets worse, we will join you."

I knew I had no choice. I looked around the cramped hut, then grabbed a small travel bag and stuffed two shirts and a pair of trousers in it. There was not much that I needed to take with me. I was wearing jeans and a T-shirt. I put on a large overcoat for the rain and stood up. All the while Johnny and Luambo were silently observing me.

Luambo walked to the door. He looked outside. It had stopped raining. Cold air blew into the hut. I tucked the coat around me.

"Time to go," Luambo said.

I knew what was going on in their minds. We had spent a good part of our lives together. It was hard to be separated now.

I took the rucksack and followed him outside. Johnny came up behind me and pulled the door closed. He left the lamp burning. It would burn until the kerosene ran out; nobody would come back to that hut again.

We fell into a single file as we went down the town paths toward the cemetery. Luambo was keeping the pace, stopping from time to time to check the road ahead. When he stopped, we all knelt down and waited for his signal to move on. We did not want to risk the chance of bumping into one of their night patrols. Because of the curfews, anyone caught out at night was charged with illegal movement. The occasional rulebreakers were mostly drunkards. In the morning, they were paraded in front of the police station, their heads shaven clean, and made to clean the toilets.

Luambo led us through the farthest end of the graveyard, on the road that led to the river. The graveyard had no fences; it was bushy, with small paths that zigzagged between the graves. The graves themselves were arranged haphazardly. People had erected fences and big crosses around some of them; in the dark, they looked like dancing figures. Rats scrambled from our path and into the bush farther away.

As we approached the river, a beam of light flashed twice from the direction of the mango trees. Luambo waved to us and we dropped down, quietly. He waited. The light flashed again.

"That's the signal," Luambo said. "Let's go."

I followed him, and Johnny fell in behind me once again.

Three big men appeared a moment later. They shook our hands without saying a single word. One of them motioned me into the canoe they'd pulled up by the shore. I hesitated, then turned around, toward my two friends.

"We shall meet again, brothers," I said quietly. The silence was too much. The only other sound was the slow movement of the water in the river as it splashed against the banks.

"Of course we shall," Luambo said. "But there is no going back now. You have to hurry."

I gave each one of them a hug and turned toward the waiting canoe. One man helped me on, and the others sat down at the tip. Using a long oar, the first man started to paddle us away from the bank.

From the canoe I could barely see the silhouettes of my two friends as they disappeared into the darkness.

Half an hour later, I was across the river, on a small rising hill that, during the day, would have given me a beautiful view of Juba. But not tonight. The darkness was complete. Would I be able to see my family again, I wondered?

A single gunshot broke the stark silence. I turned my back and followed my guides into the darkness. The rain had started again. I knew one thing: I would be back one day.

PORT SUDAN
JOURNAL

by VICTOR LUGALA

The bus pulled to a halt at the station a few minutes past nine. Port Sudan was dark and humid. I was exhausted from the twelve-hour journey from Khartoum, and now I was in a new world altogether. I needed a cold shower, but there was no public shower in sight. The air was still, and the palm trees looked like junk-metal statues. I sat on a wooden bench, deciding it would be my bed for the night.

The Red Sea was a kilometer or so away. Against a hazy background like a dull watercolor painting, I could see the silhouette of ships' masts, standing still. Modern Arabic music blared from a cassette player in a nearby restaurant.

I could see people eating there, through the large, open windows: men clad in white jallabia robes, taking in their late-evening meal. I envied them. Some of these late eaters could be night workers in the factories, or bachelors too lazy to cook for themselves, or travelers, or late arrivals like me. Smoke spiraled up from the coal in the restaurant's firepit. I imagined they were roasting goat heads. The aroma reminded me of my home, hundreds of miles away, in South Sudan.

I was too broke to afford a meal. I knew that all the money I had in the world was just enough for me to board a commuter bus, a rickshaw, or maybe a donkey. But what I didn't know was where I would go.

A man who looked like a traveler sat down near me. Despite the night, he had on dark glasses. Maybe he had a problem with his eyes? Maybe he was a thief, or a spy? There were many of them working for the new regime. I pulled my small luggage closer to me.

I was twenty-five years old. Out of college. Out of work. I was broke, living rough, and trying to explore the world. That black rucksack contained my few belongings: a pair of blue jeans, a brown T-shirt, flip-flops, three worn-out pairs of boxer shorts, a toothbrush, a comb, five novels, a pencil, and my diary. The diary had been a birthday present from my Ugandan friend, given to me before I'd left home. It was as if he knew that one day I would be far away, wandering without a destination in mind.

Behind me I had buried my past. In front of me was an abstract painting that I was to decipher while I was still stupid enough and strong enough to do it. I was in Port Sudan looking for my uncle.

"Traveling late?" the stranger in the dark glasses asked

me. He had a booming, baritone voice. Sudanese make friends easily, even with the devil.

I looked at his face, but I only saw the dark lenses. I didn't think I would be able to recognize him if I met him in a bread queue the following day.

"I'm not traveling," I lied.

He turned his face in the direction of the port and the police station; the Sudanese flag hovered on its roof. As if pricked by a pin, he twisted his body slowly like a spring, and slapped his left shoulder blade with his right paw. I cringed as if his hand had landed on my cheek. He did not bother to see if he had killed the parasite that fed on him.

"Are you expecting a visitor on the next bus?"

"No," I said.

I was hungry and tired. I was not in the mood for conversation with a stranger.

"I don't mean to pry," he said, "but when I saw that you were alone, I decided to come and speak with you. I live in the suburbs. You look like a stranger in this town. Are you not?"

I decided to tell him the truth.

"I arrived from Khartoum this evening. I don't know how to find my way to my uncle's."

Immediately, I regretted telling him so much. If he was indeed a thief, then here I was setting myself up as a soft target.

The man's face turned in my direction, but through his glasses, I couldn't tell if he was looking at me. A fat white cat mew-mewed its way past us and headed in the direction of the restaurant.

"Where does your uncle live?" the man asked.

"I really don't know much about him."

"Do you have a place to spend the night?"

I kept quiet for a few seconds.

"Right here," I said. "On this bench."

The man was silent for some time.

"This place is a den of thieves and sea jinn," he said.

I recalled the cat that had just passed by. I recalled the stories I used to hear back home, of spirits moving among mortals in the form of cats. I was scared. I was scared of this man whose eyes were concealed. Maybe he was a phantom himself.

The man dug his hand into his right shirt pocket and fished out some money. Without looking or counting, he gave the money to me.

"You should find a cheap guesthouse and something to eat," the man said. "Go in peace."

Then he left. I decided to keep the money for a darker day.

I was scared by what the man had said about thieves and sea jinn roaming the city at night, so I decided to spend the night at the police station. The first person I met there was the superintendent, and I addressed myself to him in a confessional fashion: I have just arrived from Khartoum...

Before I could finish my rehearsed statement, the man, whose eyes were heavy with sleep, interrupted.

"So what?" he said.

So far, so good, I thought. "I want a place to spend the night."

The man looked at me and at my luggage.

"We have a lot of space in the cell," he said. "Free of charge." Then he laughed sarcastically.

I stared at him.

"All right," he said. "Behind that water tank, over there."

I joined an army of street children who snored on the sand within the police compound. I rested on my back, using my luggage as a headrest. I was exhausted, and all I wanted was some sleep. I gazed at the limitless, starry sky. Where was God hiding in that endless expanse? I counted the stars until I dozed off.

Allah Hu Akbar! Allah Hu Akbar! The man of Allah woke me at dawn. I rubbed the dust from my body and proceeded to the tap to wash away the sleep from my eyes. There was a leftover stick of a cigarette in my pocket. I lit it and waited for the sun to appear.

Port Sudan town—an ancient mosaic of architecture. Thick, stone-walled fortresses, mosques with leaning minarets, a cathedral with a gong as big as a beer drum, dark mansions with cobwebbed balconies overlooking the dark-blue Red Sea. I wandered the streets, hoping to be led to a place I would temporarily cherish as home.

I passed men clad in jallabia robes soiled with red dirt as if they had rolled in a heap of snuff. Men with long, curly hair—sculptured wooden combs engraved with Arabic calligraphy projected from their manes like antennas. They chewed the twigs they used for cleaning their teeth and spat with abandon. They squinted and spoke in their own mother tongue. And they were proud in their ruggedness. I asked for directions.

Take that green and red bus, they said. It will take you straight to where your people live.

*　　*　　*

When I arrived, I found a sprawling slum: makeshift shacks, seedy alleys, valleys dotted with fresh and dry cakes of shit, skinny, bare-chested kids in tattered clothes, an open-air market buzzing with green flies, dump heaps suffocating with rot, scavenger dogs and cats sleeping in the shade of kiosks, donkeys carting drums of saline drinking water. Smelly, severed goat heads with gnashed teeth roasted on a hot grill.

The smell of poverty pervaded and perverted the mind. I trailed behind a man who had volunteered to be my guide. His hair was unkempt and dusty, and his unwashed and crumpled clothes smelled of stale sweat and dirt. His muddy feet felt unwelcome in a pair of flip-flops that did not match. He stopped to beg for a pinch of snuff from another slum-dweller with a protuberant lower lip that held a ball of quid. They exchanged pleasantries and spat in parallel directions.

"I'm taking this visitor to Juma," the escort said. "He came from Juba—sorry, I meant Khartoum."

"Welcome to Port Sudan, man. And feel at home," said the other man, extending a hand and displaying its network of bulging veins.

As we approached a dingy kiosk, a simple structure of soft wood and cardboard plastered with posters of European soccer stars and anti-polio campaigns, I could hear the singing of a sewing machine. The sound evoked distant memories of shop verandas in Juba, of sewing machines pedaled by home boys brought up on cassava and bush meat.

My guide stood in front of the kiosk. He looked at the

man behind the sewing machine and then smiled in my direction.

"Juma, I bring you a visitor from Khartoum."

The tailor jutted his head out of the window of the kiosk like a man peeping out of a moving train. Our eyes met, and then we exchanged smiles.

"Son of my brother, welcome to salty Port Sudan."

He jumped out of the kiosk, embraced my small frame, and shook my hand vigorously. I forgave my uncle for the forceful handshake, for he knew not that I was starving. Maybe this was how folks here greeted people.

As we got into some small banter, my escort waited impatiently, shifting from one leg to the other. I didn't know what he was waiting for until I saw my uncle dig his hand into his trouser pocket. When he removed it, he squeezed something into the guide's dirty palm. Without a word of good-bye, the man went to enter a dingy, make-shift building with a porous fence. I could hear murmurs, the laughter of women, and masculine voices arguing. Some of the people who emerged from there moved with unsteady steps.

This was the way of life here. And if you lived here or at the periphery of the slum, you learned to live that way. The slum-dwellers drank to drown their sorrow. Men drank, women drank, and even children drank. They drank merisa—a fermented brew that came in buckets, scooped up with small bowls or calabashes.

I blended in with everything within a few months. I woke up around six in the morning, joining the early risers in the slum, went down to the cobbled valley, unzipped my pants to my knees, and relieved myself like everyone. Women with assorted complexions also relieved themselves here. We used all sorts of wipers for cleaning up: rough cement, paper bags, newspapers, water, stones, twigs.

Relieving oneself in the open, in commune with nature—this experience in itself was almost pleasant. At night, the valley turned into a den of fornicators and drug abusers.

I became part of the slum community. I painted pictures to illustrate the dangers of the major twin killers in the area: malaria and HIV/AIDS. Then I found a job at a tire factory. I hated the menial work, and I was told that the carbon monoxide shortened people's lives, but I loved the money.

I organized a strike, so I was fired. I took my last pay and threw it into the lap of a Nubian woman whose artificial hair tickled the valley separating her nipples. Her smoke-filled home was like a crèche. She had several kids from different men who were tax evaders. They gained nothing and lost nothing. She took my money and lectured me on the New Testament.

One day I went to play cards at the community center. That lucky afternoon, I won the game, which earned me a little cash. I bought a sandwich and some cigarettes. I ate the snack and planned to smoke when I got home.

My uncle was still at the kiosk, enjoying the singing of the sewing machine. When I parted the gunnysack curtain of our home's entrance, the cardboard door was ajar; the padlock lay on the dirt floor. I entered the shack and nearly fainted. The room was swept clean of all our belongings. "Shit! Shit!" I shouted at the top of my voice. I had nothing but the jeans and worn-out T-shirt I was wearing.

After the theft, the Nubian woman wanted to take me under her wing, but I refused. I wanted independence. I wanted to go away, far away from this life of grinding poverty and the mayhem of the slum. I wanted to break free from this open prison.

The year was 1990. I remember it vividly, because Nelson Mandela was a free man. Or rather, the year I remember, but not the month, nor the day of the week. I had lost all sense of time. I was broke, starving, dreaming of nothing. I was trapped in a time warp.

It was a quiet evening, and humid. I was sitting by the Red Sea. I threw pebbles into the transparent waters, counting my age backward, but the past was irretrievable. My memories were corrupted, and I would need to restart my life. I looked straight into the horizon, and saw a tired ship groaning with cargo flying a strange flag. The ship would proceed southward, to Mombasa, Maputo, Port Elizabeth, and then back to Port Said and onward, rotating around the world. Maybe that was the ship that would bear me somewhere new, or toss me overboard. I could drift on the back of a shark that would transport me to Calcutta or even Papua New Guinea, to be initiated into the black brotherhood by eating termites and herbs.

I'll camp here tonight, I told myself. And when the tired ship docks and is relieved of its cargo, I'll pretend to be a ship cleaner. That would be the opportunity for me to slip in and hide in the hold among the rats, cockroaches, spiders, and spirits of the sea.

Darkness embraced the water, except for the beacons in the distance. Behind me lay the sleepy city twinkling with bulbs of dull colors. Pangs of hunger began to torment me. The menacing buzz of mosquitoes hummed in my ears, filling me with thoughts of malaria. I trudged back to the city, forcing along my light frame.

I decided to pass by the Merreikh Football Club to play dominoes or cards for money. If I won, I would have some beans and a piece of bread; if I was lucky enough, I would drink some tea.

I hated playing dominoes with those Bedouins, I must confess. They continually insulted me. Sometimes I imagined cutting off their large ears, which stuck out like artificial appendages. I thought of how those chaps would look without their ears. Like chickens without wings.

The club was full that night. When a good number of ships docked at the port, they brought cargo and sailors and money and diseases. I signed up for a game and went to sit on a rickety wooden bench to watch TV. There wasn't much on except for the usual religious sloganeering, propaganda, and Egyptian soaps. I was fed up with it all. I eyed the steaming metal pot of horse beans near the cashier's table. My mouth watered. The cashier stood by, counting a wad of worn-out, oily banknotes. I envied his position. He didn't sleep on an empty stomach.

Although the bulbs glowed dimly, my eyes fell on a crumpled piece of something that looked like a dry leaf. Or was it a piece of cloth, or a talisman? The harder I looked, the more it resembled a wallet. My mouth went dry. I walked over to the cashier's table. He was busy arranging his wad of money like a pack of cards. I stood before him, pretending I intended to buy some food. I dug my right hand into my empty pocket and removed it with a clenched fist.

"Oops," I exclaimed, pretending my money had fallen into the sand. I bent over the object I saw before me, grabbing it with a shaky hand. It was indeed a wallet. I didn't want to know who might have lost it. I straightened myself up and looked directly into the eyes of the cashier, who seemed to not have noticed a thing.

"Maybe I'll eat after my game?" I said aloud, to no one in particular, although I really wanted the cashier to hear it. Then I left, trying to be quick but look casual. I would not be playing any games.

I entered Abbas Restaurant and went straight to the toilet. I looked around at the four walls, painted with murals of shit. Then I reached for my trouser pocket and fished out the slim leather wallet. I held my breath and opened it.

My eyes popped out when I saw the contents: an American hundred-dollar bill, and a color passport-size photograph of a young woman with an aquiline nose, thin lips, and heavily lined eyebrows. Her hennaed hair was half covered with a white veil. Even if she was just an image, for me she was God-sent.

However, what saddened me most was the dollar note. I was broke and badly needed money, but it was not American money I was looking for. Carrying that bill would be like walking with death in my pocket. It was a curse. If the state security agents caught me with it, they would send me to the gallows without giving me a chance to tell them how I'd stumbled on the money in the first place. I would be labeled an agent of imperialism, colonialism, Americanism, and every other ism you could think of.

*   *   *

There was a feast at the Nubian's place. Three of her boys had undergone circumcision that morning. The cut had nothing to do with a rite of passage; it was simple hygiene. Even men who had not been circumcised when they were boys were now going to the hospital to reduce their chances of getting HIV.

In the backyard, Nubian women were out-cooking one another and gossiping about the occasion. Circumcision is good for men. It's healthy. A circumcised dick is better than one with a hanging forehead. Me, I can't sleep with an uncircumcised man. Sister, a dick is a dick, circumcised or not. I just can't sleep with a dirty, uncircumcised thing. Look at this penis discriminator!

The women went on. Rania, don't be ignorant. Haven't you heard that AIDS lurks in the loose skins of uncircumcised dicks? They all laughed as the delicious aroma of food escaped from around them: sizzling onions, assorted spices, peanut butter, barbecue.

The weather was stifling. Everyone was sweating, and it was worse for the women who were cooking the food. They sweated profusely, yet continued to crack salacious jokes.

The men, on the other hand, were discussing matters to do with the security of the slum. They were not talking about thieves or rapists or con men; they were talking about the police. The previous morning a truckload of officers had descended on the neighborhood in one of their regular sweeps across the city.

I'd sworn they wouldn't get any clue to where I hid my hundred-dollar bill. I had folded it into a bit of polyethylene and sewed it into the waist of my jeans. All the same, the previous day I had panicked just like anyone else.

The Nubian woman was an illicit beer queen. Since she'd gotten into the business almost a decade ago, she had been bailing out other women, but she had never landed in jail herself for possessing or selling illicit drinks. Some women whispered that she had a charm that kept the police at bay. But the truth is that she was smart, and had connections with the powerful people of the law: army officers, police officers, customs officers, port officials.

The circumcised boys sat on a mat. They wore loose calico robes. They ate cakes and candies to assuage the pain of their wounds. They enjoyed the company of the other kids from the neighborhood, talking in low tones and giggling. Their mother, the Nubian woman, coordinated the agenda of the occasion, moving from the makeshift kitchen in the backyard and giving orders to the young ladies to supply the men in the shade with more free beer.

It was an afternoon of eating, drinking, talking, and laughing. All of the visitors had kind words for the Nubian. They praised her for being a successful single mother. She was lavished with compliments for the food and beer, all free of charge and all delicious. I was even given a packet of Benson & Hedges cigarettes.

Then there was a dance that lasted until the wee hours of the night. The men beat drums improvised from tins, benches, and chairs. The women sang and thumped the ground with their feet, enticing the men with a suggestive dance. With their braids and artificial hair extensions, they swung their heads left and right, their hair hitting their shoulders while their palms worked on their bums, imitating a drumbeat. They produced a rhythm that sent the men into a frenzy.

The roosters were about to crow when I finally made my way home. When I woke up the following morning, my head pounded; I didn't have an appetite, and each time I belched there was an unpleasant smell of rotten egg in my mouth. I was constipated. When the Nubian woman sent for me, I forced myself to take a bath. I never knew why she had failed to maintain a husband; this woman knew everything to do with beer and hangovers and taking care of men, and she had prepared a breakfast for me. I ditched the solid food and concentrated on the green peppered-goat-leg soup. Sweat exploded from my forehead. I felt alive again.

I hopped from one backbreaking job to another just to keep afloat. Our people say, "It's work that makes a man what he is"; I had purged myself of all shame to do these odd jobs. The fact that Port Sudan was at the edge of the Red Sea was enough to convince me that I had hit a dead end.

At other times, though, I imagined I was a protagonist in a motion picture: Rambo, James Bond, Jackie Chan. Someone that had to beat all the odds to emerge a hero. Patience and determination kept me moving from one day to the next, hoping against hope.

Beginning in the morning and until around 2 p.m., I washed cars at the beach. In the evening, I taught a Beja revolutionary the English language. He wanted to learn it to equip himself in case the BBC asked him for an interview, and in order to haggle for arms on the black market. The more I washed those cars and taught the Beja man, the more I became disgusted with myself, the system, the government—disgusted with everything.

But this anger could be quelled by a cup of spiced

coffee brewed by the Beja man himself. After the lessons, we sat at the coffee shop overlooking the Koranic school and listened to the shrill voices of the children chanting verses and committing them to memory. After several cups of black coffee, I would excuse myself, and my pupil would take up an urn to wash his hands, face, and feet in preparation for the evening prayers.

A military junta overthrew the government. Sugar and bread queues grew longer by the day, and casual jobs became scarce. Breadwinners struggled to make ends meet. Those who couldn't get jobs as dockworkers or in the factories went to work in the agricultural operations to the south. One popular operation was called Salum (likely a corruption of Shalom), a one-time colonial post. Salum was like a hippie village: farmhands smoked pot, drank alcohol, and went to bed with the prostitutes who bootlegged the liquor.

I found work there as a farmhand growing animal fodder. It was a relief to get lost in the wilderness, far away from the real world. I buried my head in manure, plowed my plots, and soaked my skin in the saline well. We ate dry fish and okra and washed it all down with Ethiopian coffee. We played dominoes by moonlight and slept on gunnysacks like prisoners.

One day I received a letter. I never wrote nor received letters; I immediately suspected that this one might have been an arrest warrant. The new government's security agents had been cracking down on drugs and counterfeit goods, and on unwanted currencies like the hundred-dollar bill in my possession; maybe they'd gotten wind of what

I had. But who gave them the lead?

The bearer of the letter was a fellow farmhand. It had been given to him by a woman in a local bar back in the slum a week earlier; he said that she had told him that the letter was very urgent. I tore open the envelope, unfolded the letter, and read it. It had been scribbled out in an unsteady handwriting. It said my uncle Juma was very ill.

I dropped my head. I had a strange feeling that I couldn't explain, and my worry was heightened when I thought of what might have happened in the week it had taken the letter to reach me. But what worried me most was the message from the same man telling me that the woman who had given him the letter had told him that somebody else was desperately looking for me. I didn't sleep that night.

Early the next morning, I removed the American money from the waist of my jeans, wrapped it in another polyethylene bag, and put it into an old bottle of jam I had been using as my salt container. I was anxious to go and see my ill uncle, but at the same time, I couldn't shake my fear of being arrested for being in possession of American money. I closed tight the lid of that bottle and buried it in my shack. Then I left for the slum.

I made the one-hour journey in the bed of a Toyota pickup. When we reached the slum, I decided I would stop at the pharmacy to get some drugs for Uncle Juma, despite the fact that I didn't know what he was suffering from. In the end I bought some painkillers, just in case he needed them.

As I rushed home, I was aware of people peeping through the slits of their bush fences. They looked at me and whispered to each other. I didn't know whether they

were talking about me or their own affairs. At the corner
by the bakery, I met the man who had escorted me to Uncle
Juma when I'd first arrived. He looked at me and I could
see his eyes turning moist. He didn't shake my hand, but
put both his hands together with the open palms facing
upward. Muslims do this to express condolence.

I was seized with panic. He told me that they had
buried Uncle Juma the day before. He held me by the hand
and escorted me home. When the women recognized me,
they started wailing. I threw down my small bundle of
clothes and burst into tears.

Uncle Juma had died alone in his sleep. He had become
too ill to go to the hospital. He left no will, uttered no last
word to anyone.

After my uncle's death, I wanted to start a new chapter in
my life. I felt very lonely, but I had yet to decide in which
direction to put my foot.

One day I went into town to catch up with the latest
news and job opportunities, and to eavesdrop on the rumor
mill in case the ban on the dollar had been lifted. I decided
to visit one of the tailors I knew.

Before we could finish with our pleasantries, he told me
that somebody had been looking for me. He said the man
had claimed I was related to him. I made it known to the
tailor that the only relation I had in Port Sudan was dead.

"What is the name of the man?" I asked the tailor.

He only knew him by his nickname, Karlos.

"And does this Karlos know my name?"

"Yes. He mentioned your name."

A moment later, a man of medium height approached

the veranda where we were standing. He was waving his face with a newspaper. The man was dark, and he wore dark glasses, the ones fancied by the state security agents. He smiled at the tailor.

"Son of my elder brother!" the man said. His handshake was paternal, warm. His voice was the voice of the man who had sat near me on the bench at the bus station the night I arrived in Port Sudan, a year or so ago.

He smiled again, offering up my late father's full name. I realized that I could see the spitting image of my father in the gap separating his front teeth.

THE BASTARD

by NYUOL LUETH TONG

Mama taught me better. She could give me a glare that brought me to my knees when she heard me talk about anyone without respect—especially Mabiordit. It was Mabiordit who had sheltered us when we came to Juba looking for Jal e Jal and ended up stranded, with nothing in Mama's purse but twenty pounds and a battered Nokia mobile that could receive calls but not make them.

The trip from Panagam had taken three days. Two bus tickets at two hundred pounds each were beyond our means, so we paid a local merchant fifty pounds and crouched on sacks of maize flour in the back of his rusted Honda pickup truck. The roads were still under construction, full of potholes, and so narrow that you could nearly touch the mud-thatch huts and thorny shrubs on either side. At one point we had to flatten ourselves against the flour sacks to keep from getting scratched when the truck pulled over to let a group of Land Rovers pass. They whizzed by like bullets, darkened windows shielding the faces of their drivers—government officials and NGO directors. They left nothing but dust in their wake.

In Juba, after trekking across five hundred miles— almost the length of South Sudan—we found Jal e Jal happily married, with three children, and not in the least pleased by our presence. After exchanging pleasantries, he adjusted himself in his chair, faced us directly, and confirmed the rumor, spread by various relatives, that what he and Mama had done on the grass-covered shores of the Loll River fifteen years ago—never mind that it begot me—was *awoc*, a mistake. He wanted nothing to do with us, he said, and would be grateful if we never contacted him again. Then he rose up, fixed his blue tie, buttoned his black suit, and disappeared through the square door of the New Cush restaurant. There was nothing more to say.

All of this was fine by me. I was done waiting for my father's return from war. I wanted nothing to do with Jal e Jal—but you should've seen Mama, the grace and dignity on her face. It was heartbreaking and revolting at the same time. I wanted to slap her. What Jal e Jal deserved was a hard kick in the ass: fifteen years ago she had destroyed her marriage, disgraced her family, and deferred her dreams, all for him. Now she had discarded everything for him once again—a house built by her own hands, based on her blind brother's measurements, a world back in Panagam that she had forged from nothing—only to find that he had mutated into someone else.

Mabiordit, my dead aunt Adau's husband, was the only other person we knew in Juba. Aunt Adau had been found floating facedown in the Loll River twenty years ago, just a year into their marriage. This tragedy might have warranted an investigation if it hadn't been wartime. Air strikes and raids were a constant threat back then; death was so ubiquitous that people stopped asking how or why. Despite my suspicions about Mabiordit, we had no choice but to accept his invitation.

Mabiordit had extended it after Mama paid a woman selling mango juice five pounds to place the call to him, giving her a chance to explain our predicament. Mabiordit told Mama that he had a busy schedule; he was meeting with some important investors at the Equity Bank in downtown Juba at three o'clock. That would be our meeting point, he said. It sounded impressive; Mabiordit had been a poor militiaman during the war, whom we knew had never had any education.

We were downtown by midday, at a roadside café outside the Equity Bank. We drank over-sugared tea and ate biscuits for brunch. Then we sat on a metal bench, facing the street, and watched the city people to kill time. So this was Juba, the nation's largest and oldest city, a swirl of congestion and commotion. In places it looked like a ghost town: looking around I could see old, dilapidated brick buildings, and electric wires twisted and tangled around wooden utility poles. But the air was thick with cement dust from the construction sites that lined the streets, stirred up by workers digging foundations and expanding the thin dirt roads. This was coupled with the roar of countless motorcycles, and of the minibuses haphazardly collecting passengers. A random madness seemed to be the core energy of the city.

No wonder the littered streets, mud huts, and stick-and-plastic-bag slums were bustling with young people from rural villages. They were barefoot and penniless, but buoyant with dreams of a larger world to be part of. We had heard news of East African entrepreneurs peddling loan schemes, insurance pyramids, and housing projects, of NGOs with abundant resources and grand notions of salvation and development. The NGOs were convinced they could steer our nascent state away from corruption and nepotism, if only by holding up the warning signs:

MANY HAVE TAKEN THIS ROAD

IT DOES NOT LEAD TO FREEDOM

IT DOES NOT LEAD TO PROSPERITY

IT DOES NOT LEAD TO STABILITY

IT DOES NOT LEAD TO DEMOCRACY

JUST LOOK AT YOUR BRETHREN COUNTRIES

At four o'clock we began to look around for Mabiordit. Mama remembered him as a giant, broad-shouldered man, with crooked teeth and a flat nose and dark, rugged skin. She said that she used to like him, in her teens; he was the most courteous of the men who called on her older sister. He would come in the evening, after Mama and Aunt Adau had pounded the maize into flour, prepared the dinner, and milked the cows. He would wait in the yard, under their sterile mango tree—sometimes for two hours, sometimes in the rain—until they were done with their chores and able to sit down with him.

Aunt Adau sometimes sent Mama to keep him
company while she finished her work. Unlike the other
men, Mabiordit didn't treat Mama as the ten-year-old
she was; he gave her the same regard he gave Aunt Adau,
the object of his passions. They talked about themselves
through metaphors and riddles and allusions, drawing from
Dinka folklore and proverbs. He was the first man she had
a crush on, Mama said, and her feelings continued even
after he became her brother-in-law. It was Aunt Adau's
sudden death and Jal e Jal's appearance in her life that same
year that made her see the ridiculousness of her infatuation.

Mama was the only girl among the boys who marched six
miles a day, and canoed in the rainy season, to St. Joseph
Educational Center. The Comboni Missionaries had built
the school in the early '70s, with the intention of educat-
ing leaders for the then semi-autonomous region of South
Sudan. The headmaster, Father Peter—a Ugandan priest
who kept the school running even during the impossible
days of war—had plans for outstanding students to continue their education in Nairobi or Kampala, where they
could find better schools and earn scholarships to study in
Europe or even the United States.

Mama was smart; she excelled in math, English, and
history, and particularly in the study of the curative plants
she watered in the chapel yard. She used them to treat the
sick cows and goats she tended after school, and she could
recite long medical terminologies that she barely under-
stood. She would make up theories about how to remedy
the diseases that bewildered diviners and doctors both,
including her father, Doctor Josephdit, whom she helped

at the one-room clinic they ran at home. Everyone believed she was going to be a great doctor.

Mama's father was the premier doctor in the area, even though he had no formal training. His qualifications consisted of his wide travels around the country during the first war, his mastery of the Dinka, Nuer, Zande, and Shilluk tongues, and his indigenization of foreign herbal practices he had encountered in Panagam and beyond. Mama admired him and his profession but aspired to be a real doctor, a better one.

The other student thought to be brilliant and promising was Jal e Jal. He was a serious and reclusive boy from the swamp villages on the far side of the river, where people lived in straw huts built on thick floating islands of vegetation. Jal e Jal knew that education was what made presidents out of nobodies, and he knew that he was going to be the first person from the swamp to earn a college degree. He was going to be heard on radios and seen on TV and read about in newspapers. He would be famous. He would matter.

Mama and Jal e Jal were bonded by their big dreams. People saw them often on the banks of the Loll, reclined on the grass and reading English words out loud, words that even their teachers could not pronounce. They had no interest in the gossip circulating in Panagam, or in the latest fashions or music from Khartoum and Kampala. They found comfort in what the future had in store for them.

Before long Jal e Jal developed romantic feelings for Mama. After the break for farming season one year, he asked her to meet him at their usual study spot. On his way there he picked lilies from the river to give to her. His mother was a follower of the spirit of the Loll River, the symbol of which was the water lily, and he figured he could use the help of the spirits.

They met under the sausage tree on the riverbank, where monkeys congregated in the dry season when the streams in the forest dried up. Mama thought nothing of the meeting, so she wore her working garb, which was powdered with flour on the front. She had wild stories for Jal e Jal about the patients her father was treating—like the chief's wife, who had been having encounters with spirits that she was convinced wanted to make love to her.

After much coaxing, Mama accepted the lilies. She wanted only to put an end to what seemed to her to be a silly declaration of love from her best friend. Jal e Jal, of course, saw the whole thing from an entirely different perspective. He stepped closer to Mama, his eyes shut, reaching for a kiss. Mama took a step back, surprised. Jal e Jal thought she was teasing him, playing with him, and kept pushing and pushing until Mama found herself pressed against the large trunk of the sausage tree. Trapped, she threw a punch at him and split his lip. Then she dropped the lilies and ran away.

The next day they walked home from school together as if nothing had happened. A year after that, Josephdit married Mama off.

Her husband, the Colonel, was a family friend, and the marriage was meant to cement that friendship. Mama was sixteen at the time. The family received a number of handsome cows in bride wealth, close to two hundred heads, which were distributed among relatives and friends. The wedding was considered one of the most extravagant in

Panagam since the first war.

The Colonel was a rich man in his late fifties. He had eight wives, thirty children, and a dozen grandchildren, some of whom were Mama's age. In fact, his grandson Ater—a chubby fellow who enjoyed cattle-herding and fishing and hated walking the six miles to school—was Mama's classmate at St. Joseph. There was a rumor that the Colonel had originally wanted Mama's hand for Ater, and had only changed his mind when he saw her during his visit to arrange the marriage.

Mama's feet began to bleed on her first day at the Colonel's house. The man's huge homestead consisted of ten thatched adobe huts nearly a mile away from the water pump, the market, and the forest; she had to make four trips a day to fetch water and firewood sufficient to roast meat and prepare the sorghum gruel. She also had to fill the large earthen buckets in the backyard with enough water for the men's baths in the evening, and for the baths she gave the children. When she wasn't walking to the water pump or sweeping the compound or washing clothes, she was in the kitchen. She cooked not only for the family, which was made up of nearly forty members, but also for the crowd that surrounded the Colonel.

Her husband was a vain man. He exhibited his best qualities only when he was the center of attention. When he received noteworthy guests—the district commissioner, the local commander, NGO representatives—he put on a modest cotton robe and sat on a wooden chair under the tree in the middle of the compound, surrounded by children chewing on mango or maize. The wives also dressed modestly—scarves and loose robes, long enough to reach their feet and wide enough to conceal their bodies. Anyone who passed by the homestead on such days was invited in, at the Colonel's orders, and offered some porridge to eat or some milk to drink.

When he wasn't entertaining a guest, the Colonel confined himself to his sleeping hut, away from his wives and children, and demanded absolute quiet. The children had to feign naps until the sun was iridescent above the trees in the afternoon, at which time the Colonel would wake up, take a hot shower, and walk to the market. There, he would join the chief and his council and pontificate about the war and the village for hours.

Two months after the wedding, Mama stumbled upon Jal e Jal at the water pump. She smiled and waved, but he pretended he was busy watching some women by a cluster of trees. Mama brought the water container down from her head and placed it just outside the dirt path. Jal e Jal was a mess; he had grown a beard and a mustache, and his shirt was dyed with sweat and dirt. Where was the clean, promising future president of the republic? She walked closer to him, and could smell cow dung emanating from his clothes.

"What happened to my lilies?" She asked.

"Why?"

"I want them," she said.

"You threw them away."

"I left them with you, and now I want them back."

They met on the riverbank late at night a week later. Jal e Jal had plucked fresh water lilies for her. They decided to elope, but were captured the next day. Jal e Jal was fined seven cows and given fifty whips on his back. This would have ordinarily sufficed, but the Colonel, vain and proud as he was, wasn't satisfied. The marriage ended. All of the cows in bride wealth were retrieved. Fearing for his life, Jal e Jal joined the militia and disappeared. Josephdit denounced Mama, and the family was disgraced. Only Uncle Marial stood by her.

Around four months ago, a man selling cattle passed through Panagam and spent the night in our house. Mama made porridge and chicken soup that evening, and the traveler ate dinner with me by the fireside while Mama ate alone in the kitchen. After dinner, Mama collected the dishes in a bucket and washed them outside by moonlight. She joined us by the fire when she'd finished, bringing with her a new rug she had woven out of grass from the backyard. She unfolded it on the ground and sat down.

The guest glanced at Mama and then at me. He said nothing, but we knew he was grateful for the hospitality. After a long silence that bordered on awkwardness, Mama laughed as if she were among friends; it broke the ice. The man told us his name was Malwal, and that he was a veteran. He was from Kuacjok, five hours south of us. After the signing of the peace agreement, he had quit the army and returned home to take up his family's profession, buying and selling cattle. The work had taken him to eight of the ten states within South Sudan. He would purchase cows from villagers in remote areas, then sell them for three times as much in the larger cities around the country.

It was a lucrative business, Malwal said, but it had its dangers. A year earlier, some bandits had ambushed him in the long stretch of wilderness between Juba and Wau. They took the fifty cows he had just purchased and every pound he had saved.

"How did you escape?" I blurted out, interrupting him.

Mama gave me a look, and apologized for my poor manners. Malwal explained that an old friend of his in the army—now a captain, and a big shot in the national security community—had stumbled upon him that night and, with his heavily armed bodyguards, rescued him from the bandits. They killed two of them, and gave Malwal a ride to Juba.

This was when Mama said that Jal e Jal had been in the army, too. The guest began to ask questions. We didn't know which part of the army Jal e Jal had served in, but Mama had a very vivid description of him, which she shared excitedly. Jal e Jal was dark, she said, and his lower lip had a scar in the middle. (She didn't mention that it was her punch that had created the cut.) His laughter always came out like a storm, a burst, and often forced others to laugh.

The guest smiled, and said he knew exactly whom Mama was describing. He gave her Jal e Jal's phone number.

The man left early the next morning, while we were still sleeping. At breakfast, around ten, Mama placed the number and her Nokia on the table and watched them like she was expecting them to interact. I drank my milk and ate my corn gruel and watched her walk back and forth, in and out of the hut, stealing a glance now and then at the folded piece of paper and the overused phone on the table. I had never seen Mama that rattled.

The next day we visited the diviner to determine our chances of finding Jal e Jal in Juba. The diviner lived on the edge of Panagam, near the pasture and the cattle camp, where the Chinese in their green uniforms and orange caps were clearing shrubs and trees with huge machines

for a highway that seemed to be under perpetual construction. The diviner called the highway the beast's heel. She
believed the beast was slouching through the entire country, carrying the youth away to distant lands, from which
they returned more foreign than the foreigners.

At the door of the diviner's shrine, we took off our
sandals and crawled inside. The diviner was sitting in the
back, smoke drifting across her face, curling around the
ring of charms on her neck, the feathers in her cow-dung-
dyed hair, the twisted horns of oxen hanging over her head.
We sat on the ground against the mud wall and waited.

Suddenly, the room beamed with the diviner's voice,
welcoming us. Technically it was the spirits, not the
diviner, who saw the future; the spirits had something like
a remote control that enabled them to fast-forward, pause,
and rewind the affairs of the world whenever they wanted.
They didn't directly shape what happened on earth—
humans did that—but they could watch. The diviner was
the interface, whose role was to convince the spirits to do
so. I watched every move she made, to see how she summoned them.

The spirits disliked this kind of interruption, and usually refused such requests. Giving away information about
how things would unfold in the future was a tremendous
sacrifice for them; it spoiled the drama, the comedy, and
the tragedy of human affairs, without which eternity would
be, for the spirits, a condition of indefinite boredom and
nothingness. As a result, the diviners often made things up,
validating what the people who had come to them already
believed.

Mama was quiet. According to the diviner, the spirits had been following us carefully. She said that Jal e Jal

was being held captive under a spell cast by a beautiful and well-connected witch, and that the only way to break the spell was to go to him. Once he saw us, his childhood sweetheart and grown son, the spell would break, and he would leave his rich wife in a split second to come home with us. The diviner swore that this was true, so Mama believed it.

Mabiordit showed up in a dust-coated pickup truck. He was two hours late, and the night was creeping in beneath a horizon streaked with crimson and purple. He parked the truck on the sanded open area near the entrance of Equity Bank, where scrawny, half-naked children and elderly men and women extended their hands, begging the men in tailored suits and leather shoes for money.

He was tall, very tall, but not as muscular as Mama remembered. He recognized us, and walked over with a limp, smiling, his arms stretched out like he was coming to scoop us off our feet. I offered my hand, but he hugged me instead.

"Mony, yin ba raan ci det," he said. His breath was hot on my neck. I liked that he thought I was big and grown up. I was very skinny, true, but I was also tall, and my hair was longer than Mama's. That gave me a little bit more height, enough to reach Mabiordit's broad shoulders. He patted me on the back and moved on to Mama, who was standing just behind me. He hugged her for about a minute, and it seemed to make Mama uncomfortable. I could see her face going blank, the joy of seeing him squeezed out by the way he wrapped his hands around her.

Mabiordit blathered on as he rumbled the truck home.

He complained about the system, about how people like him, people who had fought and bled, were being passed over by young spoiled bastards with college degrees who had spent most of their lives abroad.

"Those bastards speak English through their noses," he said. "You can never trust a bastard with anything. By definition, a bastard is he who does not belong."

Both Mama and I were tired, and the heat coming through the pickup's glassless window frames didn't help. I couldn't stop watching Mama. The mask of strength and composure that she had assumed since Jal e Jal had shattered her hopes was still intact. I was bothered by it; it worried me that I couldn't see her pain.

"Home," Mabiordit said.

He stopped the car and jumped out. Home was a rectangular brick structure that looked like several classrooms stuck together. It seemed to be under construction, like the other houses I had seen during the ride. We were given the guest room: a wooden bed, two plastic chairs, a table, and a small closet. Mabiordit's wife, Aunt Achill, explained that the bathroom was the roofless brick square we saw standing in the backyard, and that each room was supplied with a flashlight. Mabiordit told Mama we could stay with them for as long as we needed.

Aunt Achill's first husband had been Mabiordit's sergeant, a great fighter who loved babies and carving toys from wood: cows and birds, figurines and deities, people making love, giving birth, dancing, shooting arrows at hyenas. He had been killed in the war fifteen years ago, leaving her with two boys, John and Deng, who were now fifteen and sixteen—the fattest boys I had ever seen. After his death, at least for Mabiordit, the war had lost its aura and larger purpose, so our host had decided to quit the army and care for the man's family.

For his generosity, we showed him gratitude and deference almost to the point of servility. Women no longer crawled for men—this tradition had died long before the war—but Mama would get on her knees whenever she served him a cup of tea or a plate of porridge.

Now that we had a place to sleep, we only had to find a way to make money and return home. All over Juba new houses, hotels, and shops were sprouting out of the bushes. I could be useful to someone, I thought; Uncle Marial had taught me a few things about digging foundations, plastering walls, and making bricks. Our house had taken around five years to build, but it was a masterpiece—oval and elegant, roofed with plaited grass, plastered with blue ash.

About a week into our stay, Mama woke up in the middle of the night. She pulled up the blanket, and woke me up in the process. She wanted to go to the bathroom.

She searched for the flashlight under the bed, and turned it on. What she saw so startled her that she almost bolted out of the room. In the far corner, in one of the plastic chairs, was Mabiordit, glowing in the beam of the flashlight. Mama composed herself and sat on the edge of the bed. I kept my head under the blanket and only heard his hoarse voice.

"Just making rounds," he said. "You know."

Mama said nothing—which meant she didn't know.

"I make rounds at night sometimes," he explained. "Making sure everyone is well."

An awkward silence suffocated the room. Those who have taken a life, or seen a life being taken and felt glad about it or thought it was right, even momentarily, could never completely be sound psychologically. This was the danger of war. It dissolved boundaries. The burden of the warrior was that he must walk with the living and also with the dead.

I stood up in the bed, almost hitting the ceiling with my head. Mama had placed the flashlight on the table face-up, so the room was lit up. Mabiordit saw me and lowered his head. Then he lifted his eyes toward me, and toward Mama.

"Better check on the boys," he said.

He rose up and walked out.

Mama kept asking me how long he had been sitting on the chair, watching us sleep. How long? And why? As was typical, her mind twisted the whole thing into something banal and innocent. Maybe he had fought with his wife— they had been arguing about almost everything since we moved in. Maybe he needed someone to talk to.

"He's sick in the head," I said.

"Don't say that," Mama said. "How can you say that?"

I grabbed the blanket and moved to the ground. I spent the rest of the night down there, gazing at the ceiling in the dark.

The next morning, all of us—Mama and I, Aunt Achill and her boys—had tea with biscuits out in the compound. The sun was hot on our bodies and drained the energy from our limbs. We had hardly slept.

Mabiordit showed up in his sleeping turban. His homemade metal armchair was waiting in the shade by the curtained window of his bedroom. Aunt Achil sent one of her sons to fetch Mabiordit's table, and the other son followed with a tray of hot tea, several stacks of bread, a bowl of sugar, and a jug of milk.

Mabiordit stationed himself between Mama and me. We gave each other surprised looks and said nothing. He poured his tea, mixed it with milk, and added three spoonfuls of sugar. He picked up the bread, half-dipped it, and swallowed it whole. He was acting as if nothing had happened, which made us feel like maybe nothing did happen, though his sitting between us was uncomfortable. His wife glared at us, especially at Mama.

Mabiordit looked at me and said, "Mony."

"Yes," I said.

"I saw you help the boys with the wall yesterday. You have an eye for balance. Standing upright depends on solid foundation. You see there?"

He pointed at the new houses with their high water domes rising up across the stretch of cleared land.

"That's what the bastards are spending the oil money on. They're building houses for themselves and for their relatives. They're building foundations for their future. And we'll not be left behind. We'll build our own. Right here. You are part of the family."

I had no idea what he was talking about. As far as I was concerned, this place was just a temporary shelter. We were going to hit the road home the moment we had enough money to afford two tickets. I knew he had come through for us; that was the only reason I was helping him and those fatties build their dream house, even after I had watched them steal cement and wood from the neighbors almost every night.

That afternoon Mabiordit came home early from work.

I was sitting on the doorstep when his pickup truck came roaring up. He parked it outside the compound wall, although he usually parked inside. Walking in, he passed by me without a word or a glance.

He came out several minutes later, with his armchair, and sat in the shade of the wall, facing the field, watching John and Deng pass a soccer ball to each other. I wasn't in the mood for soccer that day. I went inside and found Mama folding our clothes. She asked me to make tea for Mabiordit, and to try to be friendly to him. I couldn't stand him, but I accepted Mama's request. She was letting go of Jal e Jal, and that was good.

I brought the tea out to Mabiordit on the same tray he had used that morning. Then I sat down again on the doorstep. In several minutes Mama joined us.

"How've you been doing?" Mabiordit said.

"Wonderful," Mama said. "Thank you."

"I'm thinking you should get a bigger room."

"Thank you," Mama said, "but that won't be necessary. This room has more space than we'll ever need."

"Mony could stay with the boys," he said. "He's a big boy."

Mama and I exchanged glances.

"A boy his age shouldn't be sleeping with his mother."

Mama said nothing. It was true; I was almost fifteen. No fifteen-year-old should share a room, let alone a bed, with his mother. The boys' room was large, but the carpet smelled like urine. John and Deng were dumb and loud. A week earlier they had fought over the blonde girl in a Bringi cigarette ad on the TV at the New Sudan Club, where we watched DVDs and music videos. Each of them claimed that she had been talking to him directly.

That night the boys were quiet. They asked me to tell them about Panagam, and life there. I told them about the Loll River, and the many hours we boys spent swimming. They fell asleep, snoring, but I stayed up thinking about Mama. Leaving her to sleep alone felt wrong.

Then I fell asleep, too, only to awake in a dream. I was back in Panagam. Mama came up from behind me, and grabbed my hand. She was wearing her butterflied night-gown. She brought out a cloth and blindfolded me with it. I have a surprise for you, she said.

She led me by the hand through the field surrounding the house. We entered the cooking hut, and she uncovered my face. There was a tray there, with a gourd of milk and a bowl of porridge. Take it to my sleeping hut, she said. Someone is waiting there. She was blushing like a little girl.

Who? I asked.

Someone important. Go now!

Mama was so happy. I walked with the tray down a narrow path lined on the sides with palm trees. At Mama's sleeping hut, I found the door shut. I pushed it gently. In the darkness I saw the back of a man's head.

Anger possessed me. I dropped the tray and threw my whole body at the man, but he pushed me back and I fell against the wall. I woke up, then, and found myself in Juba. In Mama's room. Crouching on the dirt floor in the corner with Mabiordit standing over me.

His face had been transformed by rage into an unreal ugliness. He took a deep breath and hit the wall behind me. Then he left the room, barefoot, half-naked.

The next morning was slow. I was tired and upset, and I had no appetite. In the afternoon I decided against going out to the New Sudan Club to watch a movie with the boys. Instead I made myself a cup of tea and sat on the porch. After a while, it started to pour. I watched pebbles of rain hit the hard earth and bounce back into the sky, only to be pushed down by bigger pebbles. Soon there was a sea of rainwater before me, coursing and curving through the narrow dirt road and into the town, like the Loll River coursed through Panagam. It made the place somewhat familiar.

LEXICOGRAPHICIDE

by TABAN LO LIYONG

For Amos Tutuola

The following six notes were found by the bed of the victim (found dead). Here is his biographical background: at the age of seven he left school on the grounds that being in school was a waste of time. In the next three months he wrote articles that appeared in *The Light*, and drew a lot of deserved praise. You need not be reminded that *The Light* is our equivalent of the *Times*. For some unknown reason, he then abandoned writing, and was never heard from for quite a while. The next piece of information comes from me. I got it because I used to go to visit him. He said that he had written plenty of short stories, on the average of four in a day. Why weren't they published? Editors wouldn't dare print them. When I failed to have even a look at them, I turned to cursing our editors, who are so sales conscious and government-control conscious that they would never print an extraordinary, or extraordinarily written, story.

But he was busy, he said. He planned to become the ruler of our island—a total dictator of it. Once a dictator, he would personally supervise the writing of a Zed dictionary. Zed is the only language of our island. It is spoken by practically all the island's 125,000 people. It has about fifty thousand words. Communication between our people and yours is very, very infrequent, for no commercial or other interests pull foreigners to our island. And we are so proud, the last thing an islander would do is to leave. Even without a dictator, the island was already almost sealed off from the outside world. While in office, he would make it complete: the sealing off, I mean.

Now about the dictionary, before I forget. It was (he used the word *is*, while telling me) to be different from all others, on these grounds: it was going to be the only dictionary for our island. Everybody was to be issued a copy at the beginning of our year—in May, that is—and everybody was to use only the words (and even the grunts) printed in the dictionary, or else face death.

It would be easy to find out defaulters. Every Saturday, our people go to the market to receive their weekly rations of food. The market has instruments that read minds, and that could detect the presence of new words or different ideas in anybody's head.

At the end of each year, that year's edition of the

dictionary was to be returned to the government and exchanged for the next one. And every year, five hundred words would be withdrawn from the dictionary.

NOTE I

11 p.m. Been to the sports house today. Saw fighters: boxers. Didn't like it.

4 a.m. Had a bad dream. Dreamt was a boxer. The ordeal! First, you drive to the sports house. Second, you get in. Third, you go to the dressing room. (Wonder why it's called *dressing room*, when you actually undress there.) Those are some of the inconveniences of living in this obsolescent regime.

NOTE II

10 p.m. Was at the beach today—bathing. Lots of women, and men, too, exposing their bare flesh to the water, sun, and air! Sizes varied; shortness and height. Frankly, all those people may never be able to reclaim their bodies in the lost and found!

NOTE III

3 a.m. Feeling tired after writing my theory—nay, my gospel—went out for a walk. Slid into a room. Many people there. Music. A lady came on stage—I had thought we had no "lady" left. But here was one right on the stage. And with an umbrella, too. Walked about gracefully. Music. Drops umbrella—walks—drops hat— walks, music—takes off gloves. I wondered what. But she continued doing what she was doing. Quite oblivious to

my questioning looks. Even the dress was coming off. Her hair reached her back; when bobbed forward, it just covered her breasts, but the breasts had brassieres, and therefore, did not need concealment by the hair. Had underwear. Danced. Frantic. (Narration to be continued.)

NOTE IV

3.30 a.m. Fell asleep. Cannot continue narration above coherently and chronologically. Can remember this very well; was evicted from above house at 4.30 a.m.

NOTE V

4.30 a.m. Being evicted, walking home, halfway through the journey, accosted by four masked men. Said they have no clothes, no money, no writing things, and had not experienced the joy of dispossessing a man for two whole days. If I pleased, I might oblige them with my coat and its pockets, my eyeglasses and their handles (and their case too, if I had any), my watch, its winder and straps, my shoes and the strings as well, my socks (the holes and smell too were worth their trouble, they said), my trousers (buttons and buttonholes included) and their zip, my belt, if I had one, as that was one of their specialties, my shirt, my tie, my tie pin, my vest, and my underwear. I did not understand their language.

NOTE VI

5 a.m. Had a long dream tonight. Dreamt was in a classroom—professor (my ambition in childhood). Right there before my pupils, had a most singular intrusion from vandals. A horde of them had the guts to come to my classroom and call me a debtor to my face! Within a second they had

reclaimed every thread I owed them—every one, every piece of wood or grass they claimed I had taken. Then they proceeded to gnaw away at my skin, cubic millimeter by cubic millimeter, beginning from my toes and fingers. I felt the reduction coming inevitably. Fortunately, it was quick—they were numerous. They made a special point to stop before attacking my heart. They even took the time to draw the attention of my bewildered students to my heart, saying that this organ "could have saved me, but…" The class jeered before that fateful sentence was completed. Then they set to work again, with renewed vigor, with claws and teeth and enlarged, swallowing throats. It was an easy matter for them, passing from lungs and liver to throat and neck. When they reached my head, they instructed the owners of my busy hair to reclaim their things and go. That done, those who wanted my eyelashes, eyebrows, whiskers, mustache, beard (I am an intellectual, you should know), and any other hair on my face proceeded to take it. The skin of my face was removed (together with the ears and the nose), the lower jaws were disengaged, along with tongue, teeth, and palates. Two creatures (I think man and wife) sucked my eyeballs at a go. And then the skull was eaten away, and earthworms given the privilege to gobble my brain.

Epilogue: I have remembered a man who used to dodge paying taxes by behaving as if he was mad. He would sing a song, and proceed to drum, and to dance, and finally end by watching himself sing, drum, and dance.

HOLY WARRIOR

by DAVID L. LUKUDU

T he air was calm and dry. The sun would set in a few hours, maybe three or four, but its heat— a menace—would remain an adamant thorn in the flesh. Above, in the heavens, the clouds looked frozen, as though some silence had befallen the whole of Southern Sudan, and locked it in a deep mourning. Beneath the lifeless clouds, hordes of vultures hovered here and there, undisturbed by the rattling of artillery and the rumbling of nearby gunfire. In the distance, above the sea of green and the scattered, burnt-out huts, black smoke curled upward in almost every direction, nearly obscuring the horizon. It was yet another "dry season offensive."

The incessant hum of a Sudanese air force bomber, a Russian-made Antonov, faded as it crossed above yet again. A persistent, stale stench pervaded the vicinity; the intense fear of impending death was vivid to the two men in the trench on the outskirts of Yei town. Almost unnoticed were the monotonous mumblings of a nearby stream, and the anxious shrills of the birds in the bushes.

Osama could see that the young man next to him was trembling and sweating profusely. They were squatting in one of the two-meter-deep trenches that the native militias had dug; both men were completely contained by the hole, their heads below the sandbags lining the margin of the trench, AK-47 rifles snuggled between their legs with barrels pointing to the sky. They were in the Sudanese government's army, posted to the area to combat the rebels of the SPLA.

Shells whistled and echoed above the two men, flying in opposing directions and shaking the ground as they fell. The decreasing frequency of the government shells indicated to Osama that their retreat to Juba was to be rapid. The army had failed to take Yei town again, for the second year in a row. Osama and the trembling man, and possibly others in nearby trenches, were now on the verge of being left to the mercy of the rebels. But were they not assured of places in Jannah? And virgins? Was not jihad their only means to heaven?

Allah Hu Akbar! Allah Hu Akbar!

They had always chanted such phrases to boost morale while training in the desert camps of northern Sudan. The words had been their marching anthem since the early 1990s, during their endless convoys toward the battles in the South. The NIF, or National Islamic Front, Omar al-Bashir's military government, was the latest in a long line of Khartoum regimes to fight the Southern rebellion. The men were now in the midst of the holy war they had always dreamed of fighting. This was their opportunity to become *shuhada*—martyrs—and live in paradise with Allah.

The battle had been hot—very hot. Osama had not seen anything like it for the five years he had been fighting the rebels, the infidels, *kuffars*, who were not willing to embrace Islam, the one and only religion that had always mattered, and that would matter in the Sudan. If Southern Sudan could only be Islamicized, he knew, the whole of eastern, central, and southern Africa would follow. Sweet Sudan, the largest country in Africa, part of an Arab world!

It had been four days since he had eaten or slept in peace. Littering the nearby trenches were unburied dead bodies, some already rotting, as evidenced by the fresh maggots and the strong stench. From his experience, Osama knew quite well that when being overrun by the enemy, the only option was to keep calm. With a miracle from Allah, one could still be spared.

The vultures were already here, but the vultures were everywhere. The area around them looked like a graveyard that had been vandalized by bloodthirsty pirates searching for some imaginary treasure.

Osama could tell which side had suffered the heaviest casualties. He could see the deep green uniforms of the regular Sudanese army, the desert camouflage of the government's commando and Mujahideen units—probably donated by some Arab country, maybe Iraq or Iran, in the name of Islam, of Arab brotherhood—and the cream-colored uniforms of the Difaa al-Shabbi, the Popular Defense Forces. He had always had pity for the Popular

Defense Forces, hastily trained in forty-five days to boost
the dwindling numbers of government troops. They were
volunteers for the cause of jihad, homeless kids rounded up
from the streets of Khartoum, or young students carrying
out their compulsory service.

Allah Hu Akbar! Allah Hu Akbar!

"Protect us, Allah… Protect us, Allah…" the young
man was chanting next to Osama, his prayer beads clenched
in his right fist.

"What's your name?" Osama asked.

"Taha," the young man replied, softly, almost in a whisper.

"How old are you, Taha?"

"Seventeen."

"Seventeen?" Osama shook his head. "It'll be all right.
I'm Osama."

He felt pity for the young man. These boys should be
under their mothers' roofs, leaking ice cream down their
hands beneath the heat of Khartoum. They should not be
here.

"You can have this for protection," Osama said, hand-
ing the young man an amulet. He had a good collection of
them, about a dozen, hung around his neck.

"Thank you," the young man responded, his voice still
unsteady. He took the string, with its small leather talisman, and slipped it over his head.

Osama smiled. "They don't work, but…"

"But almost all of us have them," Taha said.

Cries for help could be heard from some of the nearby
trenches. There was movement in the bushes behind Osama
and to his left; he heard them and felt them. Occasionally,
there were brief bursts of gunfire, followed by more cries
and screams. It could be that the enemy infantrymen were

now finishing off the remnants of the government's troops. They were dying helplessly, he thought. "Allah," he prayed, "save us."

When the voices were only about five or so meters away, Osama felt strength ebbing from his limbs. For a moment he thought he was at the same level as the young recruit next to him: silent, weighed down, scared to death. But he gathered enough courage to peek outside their hole.

In his friend Faysal's direction he could see about four or five of the rebels, men in bits of military camouflage mixed with plain clothes. Osama and Faysal had fought together for five years; they had captured and lost and recaptured who knew how many towns and villages, had survived the most extreme conditions, had lived on rats and frogs and snakes when their supplies had run out. There had been no activity from Faysal's trench for about two days, and Osama had assumed he was dead. Now he kept his head high enough to catch a clear glimpse of what was going on.

The rebels had pulled his friend out of his hole, and Faysal was now lying on the grass on his back. It was not clear whether he was injured or not. He was not showing any signs of resistance.

"Are you a Mujahid or a government soldier?" a tall, skinny SPLA soldier was asking Faysal. His tire sandal seemed to be on Faysal's head, pressing it hard into the ground. Another rebel of similar build was removing some crumpled papers from Faysal's pockets.

"Are you a Mujahid or a government soldier?" the rebel said again.

"What's the difference?" Faysal asked, in a tired, quivering voice.

"He's a Mujahid," a shorter soldier assured his fellow

combatants. "You can tell by the bushy beard and the way he speaks. Dirty-mouthed bloody Arab! Do not spare him, but do spare his shirt for me."

Osama dropped into his trench. A feeling of dizziness engulfed him. When he heard the gunfire, he closed his eyes. He should have done something, but he had no strength left in him. The pain from a shrapnel injury to his hand had started to throb again. He had been one of the victims of an errant Antonov bombing meant for Yei town a few days earlier. His eyes were still closed when he heard Taha jolting out of the trench.

Rut-tut! Rut-tut! Rut-tut!

Taha's gun spurted as he charged forward, firing at the rebel soldiers surrounding Faysal. "Allah Hu Akbar!" he yelled. "Allah Hu Akbar!"

"No!" Osama cried, feebly. His voice had started to fail him. One SPLA soldier fell, screaming, and then a barrage of bullets brought down the young man.

"Allah, give me that strength," Osama prayed. He had seen yet another martyr. Allah Hu Akbar! Allah Hu Akbar! But he was afraid, really afraid. He did not know why he was terrified; was it not his choice to come and die? Was this not the right time to follow in the footsteps of his comrades? Even the young man he had thought was a coward had been brave enough to become a martyr.

They had heard his voice, he knew. He wanted to rise up and make his stand, to die fighting, but something held him down. In his mind he saw the image of his three sons and his wife praying with him in the shade of their house in the afternoon. Osama dropped his gun to the dirt and prayed again to Allah, closing his eyes as the rebels tossed a grenade into his hole.

POTATO THIEF

by JOHN ORYEM

Mama told us in the morning that Dad was on his way home. "He may come today," she said. And he did. He arrived just before midnight.

We had eaten cowpea leaves soaked in sesame paste; it made the water in the pot taste sweet like Kenana sugar. Dad found us spread out in the open, on the flat ground in front of Mama's hut, trying to find relief from the heat. It was excruciating.

We were blinded by the headlamps beaming out of his Land Rover. The lights flashed right into our eyes as the vehicle dragged itself to park in front of his room, a few meters away. Mama was breastfeeding Olweny, our newly born brother. She raised herself up and blinked in the light.

As soon as he'd stopped, I rushed to open the car door for my father. He rubbed my head, pushing his rough fingers through my curly hair. I grabbed his brown briefcase from his hand. He picked up his sandals from the backseat.

"Here, Sam! Put these under my bed."

I did as he said.

The driver and some young men who had arrived with Dad struggled to pull a wet, heavy sack out from behind the car. "Put it in the kitchen till morning," Dad told them.

I was too tired to wonder what Dad had brought from the countryside. But Grandma always sent us fresh maize, potatoes, pawpaw, and, most valuably, sesame paste, packaged carefully in a Foremost milk container. Whenever we went to our village during summer holidays, our demands were unending. She would receive them happily; Grandma loved us. We were her elephant tusks, she said. "You take my pains away when you come," she would whisper to us.

"Take these to my worms," she would say to Dad, when he went to see her alone. "They don't have these things in your town there!"

Our school was six miles away, so I had to be up early the following morning. I brushed my teeth and washed my face quickly, and packed my schoolbag with my books. I put a few potatoes in the bag's left pocket, then sewed the sisal potato sack shut again with a nail from the kitchen.

"Why can't you roast them first?" Mama said, when she saw what I was doing.

"No time, Ma," I said.

*   *   *

The first three periods went smoothly, but I was hungry for the raw potatoes. During break time, we either went to the football pitch or convened under the legendary mahogany trees on our school's compound. I had carried my bag with me to the football pitch; when I was replaced in the game, after only about seven minutes, I retrieved my potatoes and began to eat them like a goat.

Another boy approached to beg me for a bite. I refused, and then while he watched I wet the whole piece in my hand with spittle. Another boy came up and begged for a bite as well. I refused.

A few minutes later, on my way to the borehole for a drink of water, I met the two boys again. I was holding one last piece of potato in my hand. The boys intercepted me before I could take a drink.

"Thief!" they shouted. "You, potato thief!"

The shouting went on for a few minutes. It gained the attention of the other students, and then went wild. Some of the girls even joined in with the boys: "Thief, thief, thief!" My books were scattered everywhere. The footballers ran to see what had happened.

"Thief, thief! We've caught him!"

The school compound roared beyond control. Blood was oozing from my right ear, dripping on my white cotton uniform.

I was taken to Sister Appolonia's office. Our class prefect was called, and arrived accompanied by my two accusers. Upon seeing me, Sister Appolonia reached out for her notorious whip.

"What is it? What is it?" she asked, angrily.

"He stole potatoes from the school field," said Lado, our prefect.

I was already trembling, and in tears.

"Clean your face!" Sister Appolonia ordered. "Get rid of that blood!"

"We saw the potatoes in his pockets," my accusers said in unison. "He brought them from the field there."

"Is it true, Sam?" Sister Appolonia asked me.

"I brought them from home," I said.

"No, no! We saw him in the field," one of the boys insisted.

"Keep quiet! Who told you to speak?" Sister Appolonia shouted. We were all silent. My tears began to dry. On the veranda in front of the office, another teacher went to ring the bell for the fifth period.

"Come here!" ordered Sister Appolonia. I moved forward, and with her right hand she clutched my cheek and pinched it as if she were killing lice. Sister Appolonia jerked me upward and then down again until I was about to collapse. I cried like a child. The prefect and my accusers laughed at my torture.

"Go back to class quickly!" ordered Sister Appolonia.

I adjusted my falling shorts, tied the front buttons, and went with my betrayers toward our classroom. "You will see me on the way today!" I said to them, pointing my fingers in the air.

There was a lot of commotion when we reached our classroom. It was mathematics period, and everyone knew how serious Teacher Alex was in his lessons. The prefect moved me behind the girls, for fear of the harassment I would get from the bigger boys. Some of them had already grabbed at me, and others had thrown pencil dust inside my shirt.

"Thief, thief, thief!" Some kids were still whispering it at me while Teacher Alex drew mathematical tables on the blackboard.

"Thief, thief, potato thief!"

Assistant Headmaster, who was passing by, heard the noise and entered abruptly. Dead silence followed.

"What is it?" he inquired.

"Thief, thief, thief!" the other children roared, all eyes in the class fixed sternly on me. My face was covered by the palms of my hands.

"Quiet, please!" shouted the teacher.

That afternoon I was shouted at until I reached the gate of our family home. Neighboring boys who were not even at our school began hearing the news about what had happened.

"He stole school potatoes," they shouted. "He is a thief!"

In fear of being bullied if I ventured back out for a bath in the river that night, I stayed inside our compound and played under the acacia trees next to our fence. When Dad got home and found me idle, he suggested we weed our farmland along the main road. I agreed, and we went to collect the weeds and grasses we would burn the next day.

Just before we could retire, Sister Appolonia appeared from the Mission, riding her bicycle. When she stopped at the edge of the field, Dad rushed over to greet her. It wasn't the first time Dad had spoken with Sister Appolonia; he often asked her about our progress in school. I averted my eyes.

A few minutes later, when Sister Appolonia had ridden away, Dad turned to me. "Let's go home!" he yelled.

*   *   *

Later that night, after I had taken a bath with cold water
from the barrel next to the kitchen, Dad called me into
his room. I went and sat in front of him like a dog waiting
for bones.

"So you are a thief, eh?"

I kept silent, dumbfounded.

"Sam, I never knew you were a thief!"

"No, Baba," I pleaded.

"Who told you to steal school potatoes?"

"I did not steal, Baba," I said fearfully.

He descended on me with a heavy whip that he pulled
out from behind his back. I cried out, hoping for help from
Mama, who would sometimes intervene. Where was she?
Nyekese, my dog, barked as I wailed.

"I will kill you!" Dad announced, striking me again
until I fell to the floor. "You are a liar and a thief!"

Then Mama kicked the door open. Breathless, she
pushed Dad's foot from my head. My teeth were covered
with dust.

"What is it?" Mama asked hurriedly. "What? What?"

I waited for the lie to come out. And then, quietly,
I explained myself. Mama, remembering what she had seen
that morning, insisted to Dad that I was telling the truth.

The next day, I left the house early. The potatoes in the
kitchen no longer looked appetizing to me. On the way to
first period, when no one was looking, I cut through the
school field. It took me only a minute to dig up two potatoes there, and stuff them in my bag. They tasted delicious.

LIGHT OF DAY

by SAMUEL GARANG AKAU

M ayom and his roommate Akim had just woken up and were about to leave for the office of the United Nations High Commissioner for Refugees, a forty-five-minute trek, to consult with Mr. Njoroge on a registration issue they had. Once in a while, the UNHCR conducted a refugee census—or headcount, as it was known—in order to allocate their food supplies and determine eligibility for social services. When that year's headcount had been conducted, Mayom's name had been misspelled: they had marked him down as "Mayan," a slight mistake that could negatively impact his eligibility.

As Mayom was waiting for Akim outside the hut, he

heard a soft rumbling noise. At first, he was taken aback by it. But when he looked in the direction of the sound, he saw it for what it was: a bundle of yellow-colored water cans bouncing up and down, left and right, knocking rhythmically against each other. And then he saw the girl behind all that drama.

She was a girl of considerable height, dark and smooth-skinned. He could only gaze sheepishly as he watched her walk toward the water pump, with that bundle of yellow jerricans slung from her shoulders. She was unsuspecting, totally immersed in her own thoughts. Her hips, slightly burdened by the empty water cans, kept swaying left and right. Mayom thought she was the most phenomenal woman he had ever seen.

For a moment he stood restlessly by his hut, unable to make up his mind: should he put off the trip to the UN office so that he could pursue her that day? Mayom summoned Akim out of the hut, stressing the urgency of the matter. When Akim stepped outside, Mayom pointed at the girl and asked his friend what he thought of her.

"Honestly," Akim said. "I think she is a bomb. A rare type!"

"You think so?" Mayom said. He brightened.

But seeing that Mayom was greatly pleased by the compliment, Akim retracted his words, saying, "You have no clue of what I am getting at, dummy."

"What is it you are getting at, then?" Mayom eyed him. "You are not jealous, are you?

"Not at all. In fact, far from it."

"Good," Mayom said, gnawing his tongue, something he habitually did when he was deliberately stepping on someone's balls just a bit. "What, then?"

"What I meant by her being a 'rare type' was that—
damn, you should know this, dummy!"

Akim's tone had forced Mayom to fold his arms, sighing
apprehensively. Seeing that he was close to achieving his
purpose, Akim continued.

"She's one of those top-notchers who literally have
no time to waste. Except maybe with boys whose fathers'
names have got some silver linings."

Mayom's apprehensions had become even more pro-
nounced. Akim carefully concealed his teeth and went on.

"But, hey, my man, if you will try your best to nag her
constantly—and if she might at least make you her bush-
man, or something—hell, man, you've got to shoot for it!"

"So you will cross fingers for me?"

"Oh, sure. That won't cost me a cent."

Then, in their everyday ritual, they hugged and snapped
fingers as they let each other go.

They had to forget about the girl for the moment, as they
had to walk to the UN compound in time to have their
registration problem fixed. The boys saw Mr. Njoroge, and
all went well. They returned home later in the day, tired
and hungry.

Mayom began a daily habit of waking up very early. He
would walk around the neighborhood, looking for that mys-
terious, captivating girl. She failed to appear for some days,
but eventually Mayom saw her carrying a bundle of water
cans just like she had before. And, like a pet, he tagged along.

He quickly realized how awkward it felt, tailgating her
so closely. He branched off from their path, took a parallel
one, walked very fast until he was a few yards ahead of her,

and then cut back over. That way, he told himself, they would be approaching each other, and their meeting would seem coincidental and therefore normal.

As they came closer to each other, the girl caught sight of Mayom: a moderately tall, lean, typical Dinka boy, with clean but uncombed curly hair and a matchstick hanging stylistically from the corner of his mouth. His appearance was so his own she was totally convinced he was up to some lewd business. She eyed him judiciously but very nervously, anticipating that he would say something mischievous—"Girl, give me that ass!" or something along that line.

But it was as if he had read her mind. He bypassed her without a comment, and the girl was relieved. Then, though, she felt a little upset that a boy had passed without noticing her. She looked back, and found him looking at her. Their eyes met, and locked for a second. Thinking her stopping was an invitation, Mayom started to stride back toward her. In response, she looked down and away and began to pick up her pace away from him. He felt mortified.

Embarrassed, Mayom looked over his shoulder to see if anyone (Akim in particular) had been watching the scene. There was no one in view, and so he quickly shuffled toward his hut, afraid to look back. He entered and flopped on his bed, feeling as though all the forces of the universe had finally conspired against him.

A few days later, he went looking for her again. After a long day of sauntering in the neighborhood, he went to the pump. The girl would likely be there, waiting in the water-fetching line. Under the different shrubs surrounding the water pump, many women would sit in small groups, making quilts or embroideries, chitchatting and gossiping while the line moved forward.

To Mayom's gratitude, the girl was there. Accompanied by four other girls, she had picked her own niche. They were sitting in the shade of an acacia tree, plaiting one another's hair.

At a reasonable distance, Mayom stopped to stand gallantly, facing the girls. When their eyes met his, he beckoned in their direction. But because his gesture was not specific enough, an eighteen-year-old girl, Ajok, grabbed the youngest of the group (an eight-year-old) by the hand.

"Go tell that boy he is so cute that all of us here are fighting over him already," Ajok instructed her, in an obviously sarcastic tone. "Tell him that, in order to settle this feud, he just has to point out who is that lucky one he meant when he beckoned."

She looked the other girls in the eyes, and they all giggled. Then she asked the little girl to repeat the instruction, word by word, which the girl did successfully.

The little girl went and greeted Mayom in her most courteous manner, and told him that her name was Achol. Mayom did not have to tell her his name, little Achol said: she had heard it when he performed on Madaraka Day. Little Achol then told him exactly what she had been instructed to say.

Mayom sensed that there was a biting sarcasm underlying the message, but he was totally unaffected by it—he felt revitalized, even. He said to the little messenger, "Go tell them that I am indeed flattered, but that, unfortunately, I am here to talk to my onetime classmate—that one in the green T-shirt."

Then, feigning a deep sense of exasperation due to

his forgetfulness, he turned toward little Achol and said, "What's her name again?"

"Yom," Achol replied.

"Exactly!" he smiled, grateful for the knowledge he had dug out. Achol's inexperience had worked in his favor. He held her hands and warmly pressed them for a few seconds. "Thank you very much."

Achol looked up at him, her sweet child's face unable to hide the fact that she was very pleased. Then she ran enthusiastically back to the girls.

"Yom," she said, running out of breath. "H-h-he is your classmate—"

"Really?" Ajok interrupted, shifting her attention to Yom. "What is your classmate's name, I wonder?"

"Hmm," Yom replied. "His name is Deng, I think."

This had surely taken her some quick thinking; Deng was her best bet, since it was a most common Dinka name.

"And his father's name?" Ajok insisted.

"Garang," Yom said, laughing to mask her embarrassment.

Mayom watched her walk elegantly toward him. A feeling of victory swept through him.

"What's up, Yom?" he said.

He cursed himself over and over again in the seconds that followed. He should have started the conversation by asking what her name was, even though he knew it. That was the custom.

"Who told you my name?" she asked after a long silence.

"It was revealed," he managed to reply.

"Revealed?" She looked at him quizzically, hands on hips.

"Oh, yes. In a dream."

She smiled modestly. She was thinking to herself: if this

boy is not on the verge of losing his sense, then he definitely ranks near the top of the list of the world's greatest liars.

"So I had to track you down," he went on, persisting.

"Really?"

"Yes!" He smiled. "But the first time I saw you in person, after those torturous dreams, I felt unworthy. You were quite beyond words." He took a breath. "At first—" He looked at her palms, distracted now. A silence prevailed for a moment.

"Don't you give me that look," she said, resisting an urge to laugh again. Then she pretended she was fishing something out of her pocket and added, "Unless you want me to throw this pepper in your eyes."

He winked at her. "You know you will be the sole person to weep for me."

"So, your own mama won't even weep for you?" She was teasing him a bit.

"Do I look like a mama's boy?" He feigned displeasure; it was his way of intimidating people, of avoiding discussions along that line. He was an "unaccompanied minor," a name the UN had chosen for a group of refugee boys who had either been separated from their parents, or lost them.

"What a leap; a frog jump! De—what is your name again?" She clenched her teeth. They laughed in unison.

"Just add the letters *M-a* to your name, and that would make mine," he said finally, beaming.

"Oh, stop that familiar children's game," she said, somewhat abashed by the crudeness of what she had just said. "What is your name?"

She turned around to look at her friends, who instantly looked away, pretending they had not been watching all that time. Yom started to pick at her nails and said, "You see, those girls there are making a huge mountain out of this." She sighed. "And God knows how many thorns will be poked at me the moment I get back there. So you'd better stop taking me around and around: what is your name?"

"I am serious," he said. "Mayom is my name."

"Okay, then," she said, and thrust up her hands, utterly irritated. "Thank you, Mr. Whatever."

She had no time to play like that. Not if her friends were waiting to mock her for it.

Mayom couldn't comprehend the sudden change in her mood. Is this the way with women? he wondered. Is this why the old and wise have often warned against them? He felt a pain in his stomach, as though a flaming branch and a lump of ice had been poured in simultaneously.

"Talk to me another time," Yom said, striding backward in the direction of her friends. "And not here."

"Where at, then?"

"The water pump. Right by Deng's. Tomorrow—noon."

The following day, a few minutes before noon, Mayom arrived at the water pump. He stood under the shade of a little thorny begu shrub, waiting for Yom. After a moment he heard some voices, shouting from somewhere behind him.

"What's up, Hunter?"

He turned around and was dumbfounded for a few seconds before he recognized the two boys. They were the brothers who had beaten him fiercely at a football game, two years ago—Thon and Lei. But surprisingly enough, standing there leaning merrily on each other after two years of "no see," they looked friendly toward him now.

Ambivalent, unable to reconcile the old impression and the new, Mayom retorted, "What's up, Hunters?"

"Watch out, brother," Thon said. "If you are not very careful, those thorns will pierce your precious eyes."

"She must really be worth the pursuit," Lei added. "Must be worth all these toils he is going through."

"She?" Mayom snorted at Lei.

"Maybe not," Lei smiled.

"Then why be nosy?" Mayom tried to mask the irritation on his face.

"Why are you trying to be secretive?" Lei playfully grabbed him by the collar.

"Take your paws off," Mayom said. The brothers laughed.

While they were jesting, Yom had stealthily tried to make her way to the pump. But when she saw him in the company of the others, she retreated, thinking to herself: "Has he gone public about it? Has he been announcing it to his peers already?" Irritated, uncertain, she walked back home.

Mayom waited for another half hour with the brothers before deciding that he might have missed her while he was busy talking to them. If that had been the case, she was not to blame. But then another idea occurred to him: maybe the brothers were actually his rivals. Maybe they were there hunting for Yom, as well. Otherwise, how could they have popped up out of the blue? Perhaps Yom had messed up her scheduling, and crammed two separate dates into the same time slot.

To get to the bottom of his paranoia, Mayom decided that he needed to continue being friendly to the brothers. In that way, he would be able to eventually siphon everything out of them. Then, the next time he met Yom, he would wait to hear what her first lie would be.

"Want to go and chat at my place?" he asked his new friends.

*　　*　　*

As they walked, the boys began to tell him about how their mothers, using their hard-earned money from brewing *araki* and *changaa*, the local drinks, had sent them to a relatively well-known Kenyan boarding school not too long after they'd fought Mayom at the football match. At the Kenyan school, they said, they'd played so well on the football team that the headmaster had waived their school fees. The instruction, said the brothers, was better there than in the camp. They had learned a great deal.

But despite the headmaster's kindness, he had unintentionally done quite a few horrendous things to the brothers. The most memorable came when the headmaster addressed the student body at a weekly parade; in an attempt to make the boys into role models, he had asked them to join him in front of their classmates, Thon to his left and Lei to his right. He had then laid hands on them and said, with his thick Kikuyu accent, "If these starving refugees can lead the school team to so many victories and still do well academically, then you, my friends, who grew up eating gizeri and ugali and chapati"—he ran down the list of staple Kenyan foods—"you have every reason to aspire to the same goal, and I swear I will do everything I can to get you to it—even if it means driving you with sticks."

When Thon told this story, mimicking the headmaster's accent here and there, Mayom laughed so hard he had to lean against a nearby tree to regain his composure.

Akim, Mayom's hutmate, watched all this with disbelief. He vividly remembered the fight, and could not comprehend Thon and Lei walking together with Mayom—let alone as friends. His reservations remained even after Mayom

LIGHT OF DAY

enthusiastically introduced the boys to each other. Akim was
very anxious to see the brothers go, so that Mayom could fill
him in on why, suddenly, they were such good cronies.

It was only when, out of the blue, each boy began
talking about which girl he thought was cutest, and who
their potential rivals might be, that Akim was drawn in.
Their confessions, he saw, brought Mayom a great sense
of relief—for Yom was not mentioned by either of them.
Thon, meanwhile, seeing the promise of their newborn
circle, said jubilantly, "Me, you, you, you—we four—
I swear to God! Although I can't quite say we will be the
kings in this new game, we will show them something."

During that holiday, Thon and Lei hardly spent any time
at their homes. At their parents' huts, all they saw was repres-
sion; Mayom and Akim's "unaccompanied minor" world
offered more freedom. Mayom's pompous style of speaking
and Akim's brutal sense of humor made them feel intoxi-
cated. It was as if the whole world spun under their thumbs.

One morning, Thon and Lei came to Mayom's to chit-
chat as usual. Mayom had just woken up, and was washing
his face when the boys arrived.

"So how does that thing now stand, man?" Thon asked,
in his radiant fashion. "I mean, between you and Yom."

"Well, as you've just put it," Mayom said, "that's
between her and me."

Everyone burst into laughter.

"Forget about the way he phrased it," Akim said. "Just
tell us, fool." Then all three of them began to pick up clay
dirt and toss it at Mayom until he relented.

"It's ripe. Like you won't believe it, brothers."

"So when are you going to seal the deal, then? You've
got the hut and everything," Thon said.

"That is not it," Mayom replied. "Hut and privacy are not all you have to take into account when it comes to such things."

"What, then?"

He laughed, finding it rather ridiculous that he was being so cornered. "Want me to bring into this world another refugee?" he said, smiling.

"That is nonsense," Thon said. "Never take your Life Science classes in vain. You simply have to help her master her calendar, you know. Those of us of today's generation can easily trick Mother Nature."

"Total nonsense," Lei agreed. "The greatest human tragedy is that we worry too much." He licked his lips and shrugged his shoulders, straightening up, adjusting imaginary eyeglasses, mimicking an influential young teacher in the camp at the time, Paul Asiyo. "Can't we just live by the hyena's philosophy? Cherish that simplest of all prayers, the hyena's?" He eyed the boys authoritatively.

"Oh, cut to the chase," Akim said.

"Well, here we go," Lei said, clearly amused. "The hyena says, 'God help me get into that house where there are spoils, but as to how I will bail myself out, that I will look into later.'"

There was an amused murmur among the boys.

In Mayom's ever-calculating mind, the hyena's philosophy was very humorous. But was it persuasive? Not really. Thon and Lei had mothers and a father who could intervene on their behalf; they had a third party to help them bail themselves out. But him? Well, he could just let them do all the reckless things they fancied.

"And if you are afraid that people will enter the hut," Lei went on, "then I offer to be the security guard." He giggled. "Bring her over and I will be more than happy to shut the two of you in, and lock the door with this." He pointed at a huge padlock hanging by the door.

"And will you then shut your ears with your ass?" Mayom retorted.

"Good question," Akim jumped in. "I have heard that whenever people do that stuff, the bed squeaks and rattles and creaks…"

Mayom threw a pen at his friend's face.

Mayom's fondness for Yom began to outweigh his deepest fears; his "high-sounding" philosophies were soon cast out of the window. One day, Yom sent word that he should meet her at dawn, before women crowded the water pump. He went knowing very well that this was a moment to seize—although he was not so sure as to how he would go about it.

"Hi," she said as he approached.

"Hi," he said, rubbing his palms to warm them. There was a prolonged silence as they gazed at each other.

"So," Mayom managed to say as he moved closer to her. "Your boy is here. Trick or treat?"

"Trick," she said, her emotions becoming steady now.

"Well, you being a woman, I will take it for that which you dare not mention."

"Who taught you that?"

"I just know it."

"So, you know that many women?"

She ran her finger across his lips. His emotions rose like a leavened batch of dough, and he nibbled at her finger. They kissed and clung to each other passionately.

"Do you like him as much as he likes you?" he said.

"How much does he?"

"Like he loves to be showered by the rainfall," he said, referencing a popular song: *Oh, Ayuen, Ayuen / I love you like the onset of the rainy season / Oh lovely Dinka girl.*

"That is sweet!" she said, her head resting on his shoulders.

"I can be sweeter still," he whispered, squeezing her.

He was licking her neck while his right hand scrolled slightly down her chest, following the line dividing her breasts. She quickly but politely pushed his hand away, and he lifted his head to study her face. Her amused expression had such power over Mayom it made him want to embrace her even more tightly, so that he could momentarily feel he was a part of her; she seemed to understand this, and allowed him to bring her closer to his chest. Their foreheads touched, and they embraced again, absorbing the marvelous air circulating between them. Then they reluctantly pulled apart.

Slowly, Yom's mood began to change. Out of a strange notion, she started to look at Mayom skeptically. Inasmuch as she was drawn to him, inasmuch as she had clung to him in that dawn a moment ago, still...

Her mind began to fly forward in time. She saw their relationship continuing into the future, and pictured herself used and thrown away, like a worn-out stocking. She began to remember some of the things her aunt, her mentor, had taught her about boys.

A boy would swear his love to a girl, her aunt had said, and, should the girl fall into his scheme and sing back his chorus, the next day he would ask her to prove it. And then, as soon as he had his proof, he would quickly lose his appetite, withdraw from her, and move on to find someone new. Boys live in worlds of illusions. They are vicious.

Yom had confided in her aunt that she had met a boy who might not actually be so bad. They had conferred about him, and her aunt, while reiterating her general cynicism on the subject, had said encouragingly, "But, if you are truly blessed, my sister's child, you might someday stumble upon the right one—yes, the right one. In which case, all you would have to do is seize him properly…"

Wise as her aunt's counsel was, the fact that she could not offer a reliable method for evaluating the hearts of men had left Yom deeply conflicted.

"What are you deliberating, Miss?" Mayom said now, sensing the clouded nature of her mind.

"Nothing," she said, in a very detached manner. "But this place will soon become crowded with women, and I think you should go." And then, with some feeling for him, she said, "I am sorry; I thought we would have more time, but—" She broke off. "Maybe another time like this, in the next few days?" Her voice was getting weak.

"At my place, maybe?" he suggested.

"Oh, so that is your agenda? Because it scares me." She said this assertively and then calmly studied his face, awaiting his response.

"I don't think I have an agenda that is any different from yours at all," he said. She noticed his voice had grown tense for the first time since she had met him. And then, softening up, he continued, "If I can ever bear any evil thought toward you, it is this: to simply give you what I owe you, and to receive from you that which you clearly owe me."

"But, you see, that is the mathematical rationalization I hate."

"Well, it is simple, direct, to the point."

"So you simply want me to prove it?"

"Prove it? Oh, yes!" He blindly walked into the trap. "I don't want to hear any lame excuses from my sweet baby anymore: my hut on Wednesday night. First, we'll meet here at 2 a.m." He snapped his fingers buoyantly and started to shuffle off, purposely closing up the discussion.

What a way to reach an agreement, she thought, and then smiled, seeing what a decisive little autocrat he was capable of becoming.

The first to fetch water that morning, Yom went home happily. After finishing her other chores, she spread out a mat at her compound and leisurely sat on it, embroidering a handkerchief as a small gift—a token of remembrance—for Mayom. She would give it to him when they next met.

Thinking about him all through her craftwork, she formed her plan. When she had finished the handkerchief, she dashed into the privacy of her hut to write a brief note.

> Sorry: 2 a.m., at the water pump, is not a good idea. Wednesday eve I will tell my mom I am going to sleep at my aunt's for storytelling. I will then go to my aunt's with my best friend, Mary. We will stay at my aunt's for an hour or two, and then I will tell Mary I will be sleeping there that night. (Aunt is nicer than Mom, and will let me.) My friend will then go to her place. And around 10 or 11 p.m., at my aunt's... I will be yours.

She carefully sealed the note and slipped it into the middle page of a seventh-grade English textbook called *One More Step*. She gave the book to her eight-year-old niece, Achol, for delivery.

TALL PALMS

by ARIF GAMAL

An excerpt from Morning in Serra Mattu: A Nubian Ode

Tall palms grew high
and they were old by now
their roots stood up above
the ground in gnarled
entwine

and under one
quite lofty tree
beneath the lifted snarl

the long one lived
thick languid
quiet with
a flickery tongue

the boy never saw
the whole length of him

the house was huge
and like a palace
fifty yards in width alone
and high—the walls were mud
and then some inner part

was courtyard where
the tall palms stood
and every day
after the goats were milked
Fatima took

a large bowl full
before anything
else was done
to set it down
beneath the palm

and slowly lifting
his patterned body
the boa came
up from the earth
beneath the column
and wound himself

around the writhing root

tongue flickering
from the tapering head
he slowly lowered
to the silky drink

the bowl was empty
in a flash
and the snake
turned quickly
to the shadow

though each time
stopping once
and looking back
at Fatima
before he vanished

she was your grandmother
and written of
in the book of history
of the Sudan
as an example—the main one
of strong women who guided
men in that country
especially among the Nubian

and she was the mother
the book went on
of Jamal Mohamed Ahmed
well known by all by then

and he was your father
and when he was a boy

he never felt such fear
and such thrill
as when he followed
his mother
close behind her steps
as she carried
the large bowl
of milk
across the yard
to feed the snake
and never did he see—he said
the whole length of it

CONTRIBUTORS

SAMUEL GARANG AKAU was born in South Sudan, and is one of the so-called "Lost Boys." He is co-founder and director of New Scholars, an NGO dedicated to developing leaders in South Sudan and Kenya. He is the recipient of the Bocock/Guerard Fiction Prize from Stanford University, and the President's Award from De Anza College.

ARIF GAMAL is a poet and professor. He received his PhD in environmental sciences at the Université des Sciences et Techniques Languedocienne in Montpellier, France, and has taught at the University of San Francisco and UC Berkeley. *Morning in Serra Mattu: A Nubian Ode* is an epic poem about his childhood in colonial Sudan.

TABAN LO LIYONG is a Ugandan-born South Sudanese poet, critic, novelist, and short story writer. He has studied at a teachers' college in Uganda, at Howard University, and at the University of Iowa, where he was the first African to receive an MFA in creative writing. He has taught at the University of Papua New Guinea, Juba University in Khartoum, and the University of Nairobi, where he cofounded the department of literature with Ngugi wa Thiong'o. Liyong is currently the vice chancellor of Juba University.

VICTOR LUGALA is currently writing his MA thesis in Kenya, where he also works for the Nairobi-based Sudan Radio Service. In addition to writing short stories and poetry, he is a newspaper columnist. His satirical column "The Shoeshiners" is widely read in South Sudan.

CONTRIBUTORS

EDWARD EREMUGO LUKA graduated from the University of Juba, and worked as a physician in Darfur before specializing in public health in Germany. He was the literary editor for the Sudan Council of Churches women's newspaper, *Arise*, where most of his short stories have been published.

DAVID L. LUKUDU was born in Juba. He studied medicine at Makerere University in Kampala, Uganda, and earned a Master of Science degree in tropical medicine and international health at the University of London. His work has appeared in *Author Africa 2009*, sudaneseink.com, gurtong. net, warscapes.com, and the BBC's *Focus on Africa*.

JOHN ORYEM is a senior editor at Africa Interactive and the chief bureau officer in Sudan for Newsudanvision.com. He holds a certificate in journalism from St. Paul's and is currently finishing his MA in political anthropology at the University of Western Kordofan. He is the author of *Dr. John Garang De Mabior: In Memoriam*, *Into the Master's Footsteps: Bishop Antonio Menegazzo*, *The Bone of My Heart*, and *Amna's Tears and Other Stories*. Oryem works between Kordofan and Darfur as a Catholic priest.

NYUOL LUETH TONG was born in South Sudan. His family was forced to flee their village, becoming refugees for a decade in northern Sudan and Egypt. He occasionally writes for South Sudanese news outlets, and travels frequently around the U.S. to speak about issues both global and local. Tong is the founder and executive director of SELFSudan, a nonprofit with the mission of helping South Sudanese villagers build schools. He is currently a Reginaldo Howard Memorial Scholar at Duke University.